2

THE GUNSMITH

448

The Fantastic Mr. Verne

Books by J.R. Roberts
(Robert J. Randisi)

The Gunsmith series

Lady Gunsmith series

Angel Eyes series

Tracker series

Mountain Jack Pike series

COMING SOON!

The Gunsmith
449 – The Girl Nobody Knew

For more information visit:
www.SpeakingVolumes.us

THE GUNSMITH

448

The Fantastic Mr. Verne

J.R. Roberts

SPEAKING VOLUMES, LLC
NAPLES, FLORIDA
2019

The Fantastic Mr. Verne

ISBN 978-1-64540-066-0

Chapter One

Jules Verne wanted to go west.

Clint Adams was deep into Verne's *20,000 LEAGUES UNDER THE SEA.* He enjoyed Charles Dickens and Mark Twain and had, in fact, met Twain and become friends. But this was the first book he had read by the French author and, was enjoying it immensely.

"This isn't very flattering, you know," the girl next to him said.

He looked over at her, lying on her back. The sheet was up to her neck, plastered to the generous curves of her body.

"You're awake," he said.

She yawned and stretched, which took his attention away from the book.

"I didn't expect to wake up and catch you reading," she said. "I thought you'd be staring at me adoringly."

"I did that all night," he said.

"Liar." She pulled the sheet even closer to her chin. "I have a good mind to keep this sheet right here until you get dressed and leave."

"It's my room," he said.

"That's a technicality."

He put the book down and rolled over to face her. Her nipples were clearly defined beneath the sheet. He reached over to touch one with the tip of his finger, and then the other.

"Um," she cooed.

He took hold of the edge of the sheet beneath her chin and started to peel it down. She sighed and released her hold on it.

"Have you ever read Jules Verne?" he asked, tugging the fabric down further.

"No," she said. "What does he write?"

"They call them adventure stories, but they take place in odd locations—beneath the sea, in a volcano, underground, that sort of thing."

"Sounds boring," she said, closing her eyes as he got the sheet down to her waist.

"Well, they're not," Clint said. "It's rousing reading."

"Arousing?" she asked, with a smile.

"No," he said. "Rousing." He ran his hand over her full breasts, down over her abdomen, and then beneath the sheet. "This is arousing."

"It sure is," she said, as he touched her.

The hair between her legs was light, feathery. It took very little effort to probe through it. Her body jerked involuntarily, when the tip of his finger touched her wetness . . .

Her name was Lori. He met her on the train from Chicago to St. Louis. They sat together and talked, ate in the dining car together, then found their way to the stock car to get better acquainted. Clint tipped the stockman there to go for a walk, then made a bed of hay for them to lie down on. The coupling was quick, but it was enough to promise bigger and better things to come.

When they disembarked in St. Louis she went home and he went to the Orchard Hotel.

"I have some things to do," she told him. "But I'll come by your hotel tonight for supper."

"Sounds good," he said.

"Oh, it will be," she said.

She walked away then, her long, black hair swinging as she went. As promised, she returned that evening for supper. They spent the night together in his room, and then she went home, promising to return the next night . . . and the next . . . and she did . . .

***

This was their third morning waking up together. It was the first where she caught him reading.

He had bought the Verne book while in Chicago, where they told him the author had been there the week before and was on his way to St. Louis. He read some of it there, and some on the train.

Clint hadn't meant to spend very much time in St Louis. He had left Eclipse there before going to Chicago, so he only intended to return, pick up the Darley Arabian, and ride out. But two things had kept him there longer than planned—Lori, and the opportunity to meet Jules Verne.

He had also been considering stopping off in Hannibal, Missouri to visit Mark Twain. Then he started to wonder how the two authors would get along?

"Mmm," she said, stretching, "that's nice."

He moved closer to her so that their naked bodies were touching.

"It's going to get better," he told her.

"Is that a promise?"

Now he grasped the sheet and tossed it completely off the bed.

She laughed and rolled toward him . . .

Chapter Two

Clint spent the morning losing himself in Lori's flesh. He explored every curve and crevice of her body with his hands and his mouth, then lay back and gave himself up to her doing the same.

Why did he suspect she was married?

He usually made it a point to stay away from married women, and Lori hadn't said a word about a husband. But she went home each morning and came back each night. He was enjoying her company too much to ask her and take a chance on ruining things. Besides, he wasn't going to be in town that much longer.

Clint buried his cock deep inside Lori's vagina, and his face into the deep cleft between her breasts. She gasped and cried out as he pumped in and out of her, then went rigid for a moment before he could feel her gushing, waves of pleasure washing over her.

And then he let go and erupted inside of her . . .

***

Clint reclined on the bed and watched her get dressed. It was something he enjoyed doing.

"I've never had anyone watch me so closely," she said.

"You're beautiful," he said, "dressed or undressed."

"Yeah, yeah." She rushed to him, kissed him and then headed for the door.

"See you tonight?" he asked.

"Oh!" she said, turning to face him. "Didn't I tell you? I have a . . . thing tonight."

"Ah, well, so do I," he said. "I'm going to try and meet Jules Verne."

"That sounds . . . fun."

When it became obvious she wasn't going to tell him what her "thing" was, he decided not to ask.

"I should be able to see you tomorrow," she said.

"If I'm still here," he pointed out.

"Well," she said, "that'll make it . . . exciting."

She waved and went out the door, not the least bit worried that this might be the last time she saw him.

Definitely married, he thought.

***

After breakfast in the hotel dining room Clint went to the nearest telegraph office and sent a wire to Samuel Clemens, asking if he was in town. There would be no point in going to Hannibal if Clemens was away. As Mark

Twain, his presence was in demand in many parts of the world.

That done he had time to kill before going to the bookstore where Jules Verne was scheduled to appear. He decided to go to a local newspaper office and see if they had any back issues with information about Verne.

He found the offices of The St. Louis Post-Dispatch and asked if he could look through their morgue, where they kept copies of all back issues. When he told the attendant what he was looking for, the man helped him find issues with such stories.

What he found out about Verne was that he was almost sixty, and lived in France. His first novel was published in 1863. *20,000 Leagues Under the Sea*, the one he was reading now, was first published in 1869. The most recent articles he found were reprinted from *The New York Times*, and told of Verne coming to America on tour, and to see the West.

He thanked the morgue attendant and left. When he got to his hotel the desk clerk waved him over, and handed him a telegram.

"Just came for you about twenty minutes ago, sir," the man told him.

"Thank you."

He read the telegram in the lobby. Clemens said he was in Hannibal, and would be for some time. He hoped Clint would come up.

He folded the telegram and tucked it into a pocket. Hannibal was about forty miles North of St. Louis. He could take a train there easily, and thought Eclipse would not only enjoy, but would benefit from a ride there, so he decided to just ride there.

But before he could think of visiting Mark Twain, he had to go and listen to Jules Verne that evening, and maybe even meet him.

Clint enjoyed meeting writers, such as Twain and Robert Louis Stevenson, and was looking forward to adding Verne to the list. The last time he had crossed paths with a writer was recently, when he helped Libbie Custer research the second book she was planning to write about her husband, George Armstrong Custer. But that experience hadn't been a pleasant one. He'd never liked Custer and, as it turned out, he should have minded his own business. Libbie Custer's publisher turned out to be a snake.

But he wasn't meeting a publisher this time. He was so impressed by Verne's writing and story-telling that he just wanted to meet the man and tell him that.

Chapter Three

Clint sat in the bar at the hotel, nursed a couple of beers, and read more of Verne's book. While he was doing that, others came and went, but when three men walked in together, whooping it up because they had just arrived in St. Louis, the atmosphere in the room changed.

They went to the bar and ordered three beers, then turned to look the interior over. They were all wearing guns and trail clothes, but Clint still couldn't tell if they had ridden into St. Louis on horseback, or just gotten off a stage or train.

"Wow, this is a quiet place," one of them said, aloud. "I thought goin' to the big city was supposed to be excitin'."

"This is a hotel, friend," the bartender said to them. "Go find yourselves a dance hall and you'll see the difference."

"Is that man readin' a book?" another asked. "We're in a saloon and there's a man readin'? What's goin' on here?"

The three of them laughed.

"You don't want to mess with that man, boys," the bartender said.

"Why not?" one asked. "Is he gonna hit us with his book?"

The bartender leaned over and said, keeping his voice down, "That's Clint Adams, the Gunsmith. He's a guest here."

"That's the Gunsmith?" one of them asked, surprised. "And he's readin' a book?"

"I wonder what he's readin'?" another asked.

"Let's go and ask him," the third man said.

"Fellas, I wouldn't—" the bartender started, but they walked away.

They stopped in front of his table and stared at him. Clint ignored them and kept on reading.

"Are you really the Gunsmith?" one of them asked.

He kept reading.

"Hey!" another snapped. "We're talkin' to ya."

Clint looked up, then, at the three faces. They were all in their thirties, and feeling their oats.

"Can I ask you a question?" he said, then.

"Sure, go ahead."

"Why do idiots like you always travel in threes?" Clint asked. "Every time I have yahoos like you in front of me, begging to be shot, you come in threes. Maybe you can tell me why that is?"

"What are you talkin' about?"

"You," Clint said, pointing to him. "What's your name?"

"I'm Blake," the man said, "this is Jimmy and Adam."

"Well Blake, you take Jimmy and Adam and go back to the bar," Clint said. "I'm trying to read."

"Now see," Blake said, "that's what we don't get. You're some kinda old West legend. What the hell are you doin' readin' a book?"

"Can you read?" Clint asked. "Any of the three of you?"

"What are you talkin' about?" Jimmy asked. "We can all read."

"Well, I recommend you all buy this book and read it." He held it up.

Blake squinted and said, "Julie Ver-nay? What kinda name is that?"

"It's French."

"Wait," Adam said, "you're a legend of the old West and yer readin' a French writer? Is this a joke?"

"Come on, Mr. Gunsmith," Blake said, "show us some trick shootin'."

Clint sighed.

"You fellas should go away now." He went back to his book.

"Hey, look—" Blake started reaching out to take hold of the book. Clint was able to slam the book closed on the man's fingers, and then bring it crashing down on the table.

"Ow! Jesus!" Blake said, snatching his hand back.

"Go . . . away!" Clint shouted.

Blake took a few steps back, clutching his hand. Jimmy and Adam stared at him, and then also stepped back. The three of them drifted to the bar, with Blake still rubbing his fingers.

Clint went back to reading his book, hoping the three men had gotten the message.

***

He went back to his room to change his clothes, choosing to wear a suit to go and see, hear and, hopefully, meet Jules Verne. But the last thing he did was strap on his gunbelt. Just because he was in St. Louis didn't mean he was going to stop being careful.

Which turned out to be a good thing.

As he left his hotel he was confronted by three men, all wearing guns. It was the three from the bar: Blake, Jimmy and Adam.

"Not you three again," Clint said.

"You think you were pretty smart, closin' that book on my hand," Blake said. "Well, I gotta tell you, Mr. Gunsmith, you don't scare us."

"Is that a fact?" Clint asked. "Then that makes you three even dumber than I thought."

The men exchanged glances. People on the street could tell something was happening, and then either crossed the street, or stopped to take cover.

Chapter Four

"What possible reason could you have for pushing me?" Clint asked.

"You made fools of us in that bar," Blake said.

"Blake, you made fools of yourselves," Clint said, "and you're doing it again now. Look, I have somewhere to be, and shooting the three of you is going to make me late."

"You really think you can shoot the three of us?" Blake asked.

"What are you, ranch hands who have come to the big city?" Clint asked.

"So?"

"Ranch hands," Clint said again, "not gunmen."

"I'm pretty good with a gun," Blake said. "So's Adam."

"What are you doing here, Jimmy?" Clint asked. "If they're pretty good, let them go it alone. Why get killed for them?"

Jimmy looked at Blake and Adam.

"Jimmy," Blake said.

"He's right," Jimmy said. "We're ranch hands. I don't wanna get killed for nothin'."

"What're you doin'?" Adam asked.

"I'm gonna go have a beer," Jimmy said, and walked away.

"Now there's a smart man," Clint said. "Are you boys going to be as smart?"

"Damn it," Blake said, "we didn't mean no harm—"

"I know you didn't," Clint said. "You just have to act a little different while you're here. There are no saloons with hay and horse shit on the floor."

"Yeah," Adam said, "we're seein' that."

"Now go and find your friend and have a beer with him."

Clint could have walked past them at that point, but he waited to see what they were going to do. Finally, they turned and walked away. Clint breathed a sigh of relief, and started looking for a cab.

***

Clint had only recently been seeking out book shops when he was in large towns and cities like San Francisco, Denver, Chicago or New York. As he got down from the hansom cab on Grand Avenue, and paid the driver, he was impressed by what he saw. The shop had two large windows on either side of the doors, and they were filled with books. In one of them was a large poster with Jules Verne's name on it.

Inside the store were rows of chairs, and people milling about. Clint thought this was the perfect place for him to blend in, despite the fact that he was wearing a gun in a book shop. At least there was very little chance that anyone there would recognize him.

He chose a chair off to one side, so he could see the front of the store, and the door. It might have been overkill, given where he was, but he had already had to deal with three fools, and there were fools always made.

The chairs began to fill up, and before long there were no empties left. But people kept coming in and filled the back of the room, standing wherever there was a space.

"Good-evening," a small, appropriately bookish looking man said, coming out in front of the crowd. "My name's Mr. Elliot and I own this store. We're very happy to have an internationally famous author with us tonight. He's come from across the ocean to speak with us tonight. We have all his books available here, so when he's finished talking to us all, you can buy any one of them and have him sign it. So without further delay here is Mr. Jules Verne."

There was a door in the front wall of the store, and at that moment it opened and Verne came out. He was a white-haired, white bearded man, nattily dressed in a three-piece suit.

"I hope my English eez good enough," he said, with his French accent. "If you do not understand me, I was repeat, eh?"

A couple of people called out that he was fine, they could understand him just fine.

"Zenk you," he said, and sat in the chair the store had provided for him.

Speaking as clearly and precisely as he could, and slowly, Verne went on to talk about how much he enjoyed writing the books he did, how much he was enjoying visiting the United States, and how much he looked forward to see the "Old West," now that he was in St. Louis, about to cross the "Mizzizzippi" River."

When he was finished Mr. Elliot invited questions from the audience, and got quite a few in return. Most of them had to do with Verne's subject matter. They wanted to know whatever made him think of writing about man going into space, or beneath the earth, or under the ocean. Verne said, that these were places he wished he could actually explore, and that the next best thing was to research and write about them.

Once the questions were done Verne sat behind a table and people lined up to have him sign his books. Clint waited in his chair while the line got shorter and shorter, then stood up to make sure that he went last.

Clint didn't know if he was supposed to bring his own copy of 20,000 Leagues, or buy a book there, so he decided to buy *Journey to the Center of the Earth.* When no one else was around the table he handed Verne the book.

"I enjoyed your talk," Clint said.

Verne looked up at him, then at the gun on his hip.

"You are from the West?"

"Yes, I am."

"I am looking forward to seeing it," the author said. "What eez your name? I was personalize your book. Is that the word? Person-a-lize?"

"That's it," Clint said.

"Please? Your name?"

"It's Clint."

"No, no, I must have your full name."

And as Mr. Elliot came over to join them Clint said, "Clint Adams."

"Did you say Adams?" Elliot asked.

"Uh, yes, I did."

"You know theez man?" Verne asked.

"I've heard of him," Elliot said.

"Oh? And how eez that?"

"I'll show you."

Elliot went to another part of the shop, came back with several dime novels, all of which had been written about The Gunsmith.

"Zee Gunsmith?" Verne asked, taking one of the novels and looking it over.

"He's a legend in the west," Elliot said.

"I just came to buy a book and get it signed," Clint said. Verne looked up from the dime novel in his hand. "And I wanted to tell you how much I enjoy your stories."

"Sank you," Verne said.

Clint picked up his copy of "Journey" and said, "Thanks very much."

"Mr. Adams!"

He started for the door, and Elliot chased him.

"Would you consider appearing here at the store—"

"No," Clint said, "that's not something I would do."

"I have many copies of these dime novels," Elliot went on. "They sell very well, and my customers would love to have you—"

"I'm sorry, Mr. Elliot," Clint said, "but I'm leaving St. Louis tomorrow."

"You couldn't put that off?" Elliot asked.

"You know us legends of the Old West," Clint said, "we tend to stay in the Old West."

"But—I didn't mean—I'm sorry—" Elliot was blustering, as Clint went out the door.

Chapter Five

Clint had a quiet supper in the hotel that night he stayed in so he wouldn't take a chance on running into Blake and his friends, again. It was time to be done with St. Louis.

In the morning he went down to check out and have breakfast. He intended to head for Hannibal to see Sam Clemens later, but was shocked to find Jules Verne waiting in the lobby. The man was dressed almost exactly as he had been the night before, but the suit was a different shade.

"Mr. Verne," Clint said.

"Monsieur Adams," Verne said, "I hope you don't mind zat I am here."

"No, sir," Clint said, "but I'm wondering how you knew where to find me."

"Ah, Monsieur Elliot helped me with zat. He thought a man like you would stay in one of a few hotels and he sent some men out to check for me. May I have zee breakfast with you?"

"I'd be honored," Clint said. "I would have liked to talk to you more last night, but Elliot was getting on my nerves, to be truthful."

"I think I understand."

"I was going to have breakfast here in the hotel," Clint said. "Would that be all right with you?"

"Yes, fine."

As they started to walk toward the dining room Clint noticed that the author walked with a limp.

The dining room was only half full, and Clint was able to point out the table he wanted.

As they sat, he finally asked, "When did you hurt your leg?" because he was just too curious.

"Eet was last year," Verne said. "My nephew shot me in the leg."

"Your nephew?" Clint asked. "Why did he do that?"

"He is a sick young man," Verne said. "He is now in an asylum."

"That's too bad. Will the injury improve?"

"I am afraid not. Zee doctors say I will probably limp for the rest of my life."

"I'm sorry to hear that."

Verne shrugged and said, "It is just something else I must deal with in life. We all have zem."

"Yes, we do," Clint said.

A waiter came over and they both ordered eggs.

"Can you do *omelet du fromage*?" Verne asked.

"A what?" Clint asked.

"It's French," the waiter said. "It's eggs and cheese—yes, sir. We can do that."

"Excellent!" Verne said, with a smile.

"I'll try that, too," Clint said, "but can you put some bacon in mine?"

"Yes, sir."

"And a pot of coffee, please," Clint said.

"Strong coffee," Verne added.

"Ah, a man after my own heart," Clint commented.

"And I'll bring a basket of fresh biscuits," the waiter offered.

"That'd be great," Clint said.

"Have you never had zee omelet?" Verne asked.

"I've never even heard the word," Clint said, "or that other word . . ."

". . . *fromage,*" Verne said. "It simply means cheese."

"Usually, on the trail, you just toss an egg into a pan and scramble it around," Clint said. "What's the difference with this omelet?"

"You do not move it around in zee pan," Verne said, "you simply . . . fold it—usually around some cheese or, as you have asked for, some meat and vegetables."

"Vegetables?"

"Peppers, onions, add some salt and pepper . . . you will see."

While they waited Clint asked Verne what cities he had visited so far in the United States. Verne said New

York, Washington D.C., Philadelphia, Boston, and Chicago.

"And what are your plans after St. Louis?" Clint asked.

"As I believe I said last night," Verne went on, "I want to see the wild West."

"It's not as wild as it used to be," Clint warned him. "It's getting pretty civilized."

"I met Charles Dickens shortly before he died," Verne said, "He told me he never went further west zen here, in St. Louis, when he came to America in forty-two. But I also know Oscar Wilde, who was here in your country in eight-two. He loved the Old West, and insisted I must see it. He went to many places, drank in many saloons . . . I believe he went to a town called . . . Leadville?"

"Probably Colorado," Clint said. "There's not much there since the mines played out."

"You see?" Verne said. "Zis is what I wanted to talk wiz you about."

"What's that?"

"If I got to zee west myself, I will go to the wrong places."

"Uh-huh."

"But if someone from zee west goes with me, they will take me to zee right places."

"So . . . wait. You want me to take you west?"

"I read zos dime novels Monsieur Elliot gave me," Verne said. "You are quite famous."

"Or infamous," Clint said. "Actually, you can't believe everything you read."

"Oh, I do not believe it," Verne said. "But I would zink there was a germ of truth."

"Sure," Clint said, "A germ."

"Zen you are the man I need," Verne said.

The waiter came with their coffee, poured it and promised to be right back with their food.

"What can I do to get you to take me west?" Verne asked.

"Mr. Verne—"

"Please," the Frenchman said, "call me Jules."

"Jules . . . I'll have to think about it."

"Zat ees good," Verne said. "You did not say no right away."

The waiter scurried over with their plates.

"*Omelet du fromage*," he said, "as ordered."

"Zenk you," Verne said.

"And the same for you," the waiter said to Clint, "but with bacon."

"Thanks."

"I'll get those biscuits."

"Look," Clint said, "I was heading up to Hannibal to see a friend today. Would you like to come with me?"

"Hannibal?" Verne asked. "What eez zis place?"

"It's a small town about forty miles north of here," Clint said. "I was going to ride up on my horse, but we could rent a buggy. And you'd get to see some of the countryside."

"And when we get zere?" Verne asked. "What would I see, zen?"

"Well, my friend."

"And who is he?"

"His name is Samuel Clemens."

"And do I know zees Clemens?" Verne asked, chewing his omelet. "Is he also a legend?"

"Of a sort," Clint said. "He's also known as . . . Mark Twain."

Verne stopped chewing.

"Mark Twain?" he asked. "You mean, zee famous American author?"

"That's him."

"He is your friend?"

"He is."

"And you are going to see him?"

"I am," Clint said. "He invited me to drop by, and that's what I'm going to do. I sent a telegram to make sure he was there, and he said to come ahead."

Verne cut off another hunk of his omelet. Clint put a piece of his into his mouth.

"Wow," he said, "this is good."

The waiter came, left the biscuits and butter, then went back to the kitchen.

"So . . . you would take me wiz you? Introduce me to Mark Twain?"

"I would, yes," Clint said. "I think he'd really like meeting you."

"But zis Hannibal, it is not in zee West?"

"No," Clint said, "but we can talk about that . . . after."

"*Oui,*" Verne said, "we talk after. Today I will meet Mark Twain."

"Yes," Clint said. He took another hunk of the omelet. "This is really good."

"*Oui*, I told you," Verne said.

Chapter Six

When they finished breakfast, they went to the livery stable where Clint had Eclipse and rented a buggy.

"What about your horse?" the hostler asked.

"I'll take him along," Clint said. "He can use the exercise."

"I'll tie him to the back of the buggy for ya."

"Thanks."

Clint climbed up onto the buggy next to Verne.

"We'll have to stop by your hotel and pick up your things," he said.

"That will not be a problem," the author assured him. "I do not unpack my suitcase in hotels, so I will just pick it up and go."

"Do you have anymore, uh, events like last night?"

"I do not," Verne said. "My intention was to go west from St. Louis."

"What about your publisher?" Clint asked. "Didn't they send someone with you?"

"I do not need zee minder," Verne said. "Not when I am in a city. However, zee West, that will be different."

"All set," the hostler said.

"See you in a few days," Clint said, and snapped the reins to get the horse going.

***

During the ride to Hannibal Verne's head kept swiveling around, and he kept pointing out trees and animals.

"Don't you have trees and animals in France?" Clint asked.

"Of course," Verne said, "but not like zees. And zee air, it does not smell like zees."

So the author continued pointing and taking deep breaths until they arrived in Hannibal, hours later.

"What a lovely little town," Verne said. "Zees is the place Monsieur Twain always writes about, no?"

"Yes."

"I can see why."

Clint directed the buggy through the streets of Hannibal until he saw Samuel Clemens' house just ahead of them. Eclipse trotted obediently behind, tied to the back, although there was really no reason for that. The Darley would have followed them the whole way, even untethered.

Clint reined in the buggy in front of Clemens' house, climbed down and tied the horse to the lone hitching rail. Verne got down from the buggy on his own. Despite his limp the man seemed to be able to get himself around.

"Zees is excellent!" he said, looking at Clemens' simple house. "I thought he would live in a larger home."

"He does," Clint said. "He has a home with his wife and children in Hartford, Connecticut. And in the summer at his sister's house in Elmira, New York. He comes here from time to time to reconnect."

There was a white picket fence around the house. Clint opened the gate and they went up the walk to the front door. Clint knocked and they waited. When Clemens opened the door he smiled broadly and embraced Clint enthusiastically.

"You came!" he shouted. "When we saw each other last month in Sacramento I never expected to see you again this soon."

"Well, you told me you were going to be here, and I was on my way back from Chicago."

"What the hell were you doin' in Chicago?"

"It had to do with the whole Libbie Custer thing, but we can discuss that later. I brought someone for you to meet. Mark Twain this is Jules Verne."

"Verne!" Clemens said, his bushy white eyebrows shooting up. "I heard you were gonna be in Missouri."

"I hope you do not mind that I came along with Monsieur Clint."

"Hey, any friend of Mon-soor Clint's is a friend of mine—especially a fellow author." He shook Verne's hand vigorously, then tugged him into the house. "Come on in, both of you!"

Clint followed the two authors into the house, closing the door behind him. By the time he caught up to them in Clemens' livingroom they were deep in conversation about books and authors. Clint read books when he was alone in his hotel room, but he did not count himself a reader. So he had no idea who or what they were discussing.

"Clint," Clemens said, pointing, "I got us some good bourbon over there. Pour us each some, will ya?"

"You've got it, Sam," Clint said.

While the two writers continued talking, Clint went to the sidebar Clemens had pointed to and poured three glasses of bourbon. He'd have to take Clemens' word for the fact that it was good stuff, because he was almost strictly a beer man.

"Here you go," he said, handing them each a glass.

"So what are you fellas plannin' to do now that you're here?" Clemens asked.

"Well, first we'll have to find a hotel," Clint said, "and then I just thought you'd want to show Jules Hannibal, tomorrow."

"Well," Clemens said, paraphrasing Clint, "*first* you fellas ain't stayin' in no hotel, you're stayin' right here with me. I got a woman I know comin' in there to cook for us tonight, and then you each got your own room."

"Zat ees very generous," Verne said. "Thank you, Monsieur Twain."

"And you," Clemens said, pointing at Verne, "gotta call me Sam, okay?"

"*Oui,*" Verne said, "and you must call me Jules."

"Okay, with that decided," Clemens said, "tomorrow I'll show you places where Tom Sawyer, Huck Finn and the Jumping Frog have been."

"Zees is excellent," Verne said, of the bourbon.

"You think that's good, wait'll you taste the food tonight," Clemens said. "The woman has a restaurant here in town, but she's always tellin' me to let her know when I need her to cook for me. So I picked tonight."

"I look forward to it," Jules said.

"Clint," Clemens said, "why don't you go out and get your bags? I'll get you both set in your rooms."

"Sure," Clint said, "why not?"

He hadn't expected the two authors to get along so well so quickly, but they were pretty much reducing him to a bartender and bell boy.

But he didn't mind. These were two brilliant men, and he hoped that he was not only going to be able to call Mark Twain his friend but, after this, also Jules Verne.

Chapter Seven

Clemens' house didn't have indoor facilities, but the writer had supplied a pitcher-and-basin in each of the rooms. After they had cleaned up and changed, they came back downstairs.

Clint had put on a clean shirt, but Verne had donned an entirely new suit—same style, slightly different color.

They could hear someone moving around in the kitchen, and detected the aroma of home cooking.

"Smells great," Clint said.

Clemens was seated on his sofa, smoking a pipe. He was dressed casually, not in the white suit he favored when making appearances.

"Jules," he said, "we gotta get you to start dressin' a little more casual."

Verne looked down at himself, and then back at Clemens in confusion.

"But zees is my most casual attire."

Clemens looked at Clint, who only shrugged.

"Let's go out on the front porch," Clemens said. "Anybody want another bourbon? Maybe a lemonade?"

"No," Clint said, "I think I'll just wait for supper."

"*Oui*, I also will wait."

"Follow me, then."

They filed out to the porch, after Clemens shouted, "Emma, we'll be on the porch. Let us know when supper's ready."

"Okay, Sam!"

On the porch Clint asked, "Does your wife know about Emma?"

"There's nothin' to know," Clemens said. "The woman is a great cook."

Clint studied Clemens, then decided the man was serious. He was only interested in Emma as a cook.

There were chairs for all of them, so they sat and stared out at the street. Every so often someone would walk by and exchange a wave with Clemens.

"Does everyone here know who you are?" Verne asked him.

"Oh yeah," Clemens said, "but they know Sam Clemens. They don't make no fuss about a feller named Mark Twain. What about you, back home?"

"Ah, zey make zee fuss," Verne said. "Sometimes eet iz too much."

"I can believe it," Clemens said. "Folks in other places I appear go overboard."

"That's because the two of you are such great storytellers," Clint said.

Clemens looked at Clint, then back to Verne.

"He's right, you know," he said. "You're a great storyteller."

"You have read my work?" Verne asked, looking surprised.

"Oh, hell, yeah," Clemens said. "Journey to the Center of the Earth? Twenty Thousand Leagues Under the Sea? That Captain Nemo, he's a brilliant character."

"Tom Sawyer and Huckleberry Feen," Verne said, "now those are brilliant characters."

"My God, all they did was go down the Mississippi on a raft," Clemens said. "Your characters have gone to the moon, to the center of the earth. Amazing! And you make the reader feel like he's there." Clemens looked at Clint. "Doesn't he?"

"That he does. And I agree with you both. In their own ways Nemo is amazing, and so are Tom and Huck."

"Huck," Verne said, "yes, Huck. A wonderful name!"

"What bout Nemo—" Clemens started, but the door opened a crack and a woman's voice said, "Supper's on."

"Ah," Clemens said to them, getting to his feet, "now you will taste something truly amazing."

Clint and Verne filed into the house after Clemens, who led them directly to the dining room, where the table seemed to be covered with food.

Chapter Eight

The cook, Emma, had laid out plates of fried chicken and pork chops, bowls of potatoes, boiled with parsley, corn and carrots, and a basket of fresh cornbread.

"My God," Verne said, biting into the fried chicken, "zees is amazing."

Clint nodded his complete agreement. He couldn't speak because his mouth was so full of chicken breast.

"I told you," Clemens said. "She has a café and I eat there . . . a lot . . . when I'm in town. You guys wanna meet 'er?"

"Of course!" Verne said.

"Sure," Clint chimed in.

"I'll get 'er."

Clemens got up and went to the kitchen. He was back in moments with the woman who had prepared the absolute feast that was before them.

Clint expected a fiftyish woman, thick around the middle, with fat red cheeks and a ready smile.

What he got was a shock.

The woman Clemens was proudly presenting to them was hardly thirty. Although she wore an apron, and her hair was tied back, Clint could see how pretty she was, how well built, and knew that—when released—her hair would cascade down her back.

"Gentlemen, this is Emma Deane. She runs Emma's, the best eatery in Hannibal. Emma, this is Mr. Jules Verne, a writer who's visiting from France."

"France," Emma said, her eyes wide. "I'd love to go there. Welcome, Mr. Verne."

"And this is Clint Adams," Clemens said. "I think you might've heard of him."

"Are you the Gunsmith?"

"He sure is," Clemens said, "and a good friend of mine."

"Well, I'm happy to meet you both," she said.

"Zees meal is unbelievable," Verne said. "I believe eet ees zee best I have had since I left France."

"I'm flattered," she said, turning slightly red. "Thank you."

"He's right," Clint added, "This is the best fried chicken I've ever had."

"Thank you, sir," she said. "I better get back into the kitchen, I have a cobbler in the oven. You gents should come to my café while you're in town."

"I'll definitely bring 'em," Clemens said. "You can count on it."

Emma poked him in the arm and said, "You better sit down and eat."

"Yes, Ma'am."

Emma almost curtsied, and then returned to the kitchen. Clemens sat down, took a chicken wing. It was the only thing on his plate.

"The young lady said eat," Clint told him.

"I'm eating, I'm eating," he said, taking some potatoes.

Clemens answered many questions from Verne about Hannibal during the meal. Clint concentrated on his meal and let the two writers talk. He was also thinking about Verne's request that Clint take him west. His last trip with a writer had not gone well, but Libbie Custer was not Jules Verne, and Verne's publisher was not involved. Also, Verne had no requests as to where to go. It would be Clint's choice which towns to show him. If he took him to places like Dodge City and Tombstone, both towns were sleepy, as opposed to their wild and woolly days. But they were historic.

Where was the harm? Show Jules Verne the O.K. Corral while there was nothing there but horses. He was going to have to find out if the French author could ride, as that would be easier than trying to get around in a buggy the entire time.

"Clint!" Clemens yelled.

"Huh?"

"I asked if you were thinking of showing Jules Dodge City," Clemens said.

Verne interrupted even before Clint was able to answer the question.

"Ah, but Monsieur Clint has not yet decided if he will take me west."

"Oh, of course he'll take you," Clemens said. "What else has he got to do?"

"But I do not know, *mon ami*, what legends do," Verne admitted.

"They show other legends the countryside, that's what they do," Clemens said.

"Oh, I am not a legend, Monsieur Sam," Verne said. "Such a title is reserved for ones such as you."

"Me? Now you're really talkin' like a crazy Frenchman," Clemens said, laughing. "The Gunsmith is the only legend in this room."

"How about we stop all this talk about legends?" Clint asked.

"Sure thing," Sam Clemens said. "Whataya wanna talk about, Clint?"

Clint sniffed the air and said, "Let's talk about that cobbler I smell. I'm thinking apple."

Chapter Nine

After supper they went out and sat on the porch again. The neighborhood where Sam Clemens lived was very quiet. Inside, Emma was cleaning up the dining room and kitchen.

"Cobbler," Verne said. "I have never had that before. Delicious."

"They don't do cobbler in France?" Clemens asked, around his pipe stem.

"Many small and large desserts," Verne said, "fancy desserts, but no cobbler."

Clemens sat forward.

"You know what you should do?"

"What?" Verne asked.

"You should take Emma to France," Clemens said. "Let her open a restaurant there. It would make a fortune."

"I thought you were all about writing and publishing," Clint said. "Now you know how to make money opening a restaurant?"

"I don't know anything about restaurants," Clemens said. "But Emma does."

"Emma does what?" Emma asked, coming out the front door.

"Cooks," Clemens said, looking up at her. "Best cook in Missouri."

"I thought you said I was the best in Hannibal?" she asked.

"Missouri," Clemens said, "All of Missouri."

"Oh, it's already dark," she said, looking out at the street.

Clint had been right about her hair. The honey locks were now untied and hanging down past her shoulders. Without the apron he could see she was wearing a simple cotton dress, which she had probably worn during the day at work in her café.

"You want me to walk you home, darlin'?" Clemens asked.

"No, Sam," she said, "I thought maybe your friend Clint would escort me home."

Clemens looked at Clint.

"I'd be happy to, Emma," Clint said, standing.

"Good-night, Sam," she said, "Mr. Verne. It was very nice to meet you."

"Charmed," Verne said.

She raised her eyebrows.

"No man has ever said that to me before," she said. "Charmed." She stepped off the porch and started down the walk.

"Gentlemen," Clint said. "I'll be back soon."

He turned and followed her.

***

"That's my café," she said, pointing.

"It looks nice," he commented.

"It's small," she said. "I'm lookin' to expand. Sam said he might wanna back me."

"Is that why you cook for him?"

"No," she said, "I cook for him because I like him. I never asked him for money."

"Well," Clint said, "He likes to invest, but a restaurant, that would be new for him."

"He doesn't want to be involved," she said. "He just wants to back me."

"Did you say yes?"

"No."

"Why not?"

"Because then people would think what you just thought," she said. "That I was taking Mark Twain for his money."

"I don't think that."

"You did," she said. "For a minute. Admit it."

"Okay, maybe for a minute."

"We turn here," she said, and then turned down a side street. "I'm at the end."

They walked to the end of the street and stopped in front of a small, one-story house.

"This is it."

"Well," Clint said, "thanks for the great meal. Good-night."

He started to walk away.

"Wait!" she said

He turned.

"That's it?"

"What do you mean?"

"I mean, you're the Gunsmith," she said. "You have . . . a reputation. Am I . . . not pretty enough?"

"Emma—"

"Could you just come inside with me?" she asked. "You know, to make sure it's safe?"

Clint looked at her for a moment, appearing so pretty in the moonlight, and then said, "Sure, Emma. Sure."

She smiled, turned and walked to the door. She unlocked it, then took his hand to lead him inside.

"There's a lamp on a table to the right . . . yes, there."

He groped in the dark, found the lamp, struck a match and lit the wick. As the light bathed the room he turned and saw that she had already removed her dress.

Chapter Ten

She was totally naked.

In the soft light of the lamp her skin seemed tinged orange, her nipples slightly darker.

"I know," she said. "That lamp gives off an orange light. I've been meaning to get a different one."

"You look beautiful," he said, "no matter what color the light is."

Her breasts and hips were full, as were her thighs. He knew if she turned around she'd have a marvelously chunky butt.

"Do I look fat?" she asked. "You can't stop staring at me. I'm starting to feel . . . self-conscious."

"Don't," he said. "I'm staring because I can't take my eyes off you."

"I'm fat."

"Not at all," he said, approaching her. "You're perfect."

"For what?"

"For bed."

"I've never done this before," she admitted.

"What's that? Had sex?"

“No, I’ve had sex,” she said “but not like this.” She closed her eyes, then opened them again. “This has taken all my nerve. I didn’t know how you would react.”

“You want me to show you how my body is reacting?” he asked.

“Yes, please.”

He unstrapped his gunbelt, set it aside within easy reach, then kept his eyes on her as he took off the rest of his clothes. When his hard, jutting cock came into view her eyes widened, and she licked her lips.

“There,” he said. “I don’t have a choice. This is what your beauty has done to me.”

“I’m not beautiful,” she said.

“You’re more than that,” he told her.

They were only a step apart, but could feel the heat emanating from the other’s body. Then he closed the gap, and put his hard cock in her hands.

“Oh my,” she said.

“Still nervous?” he asked.

She looked at him and smiled.

“Petrified.”

“Do you want to stop?”

“Oh, no,” she breathed.

He leaned down and kissed her. She leaned into the kiss, and her nipples brushed his chest. He put his arms around her to gather her in close, and the kiss intensified.

"Do you think the house is safe?" he asked.

"Not for you," she whispered. "Let's go to the bedroom."

She took his hand to lead him there, but he paused to pick up his gunbelt.

"Will you need that?" she asked.

"You never know."

He let her lead him into her bedroom, turned to face him with her hands on his hips.

"You want to put that gun where you can reach it? How's the bedpost?"

"That's the usual place."

He walked past her, hung the gun, and turned.

"I'm nervous," she said. "It's taken all my courage to get this far."

"This is pretty far, Emma."

"I know," she said. "I just . . . couldn't let the opportunity pass me by."

"Opportunity?"

"To be with you," she said.

"Now Emma—"

"Look," she said, "I know this sounds terrible, but Hannibal is a small town. I have a business, and I can't be getting involved with my customers. You're gonna be gone soon, right?"

"Right."

"Would you mind if we made some memories to-night?" she asked.

"Good ones, I hope. All you have to do is relax."

She took a deep breath.

"Okay," she said, looking down at his crotch again. "I'm ready."

He moved to her, pulled her to him and kissed her, pinning his hard cock between them. She moaned, rubbed herself against him, ran her hands over his body.

He turned her so that her back was to the bed and pushed her down on it, then crawled on top of her. She caught his hard penis between her thighs, and he started moving back and forth, enjoying the smoothness of her skin as they built up some friction.

"Oh Lord," she said, "I believe I'm ready."

He pulled his penis free of her thighs, spread her legs wide and pressed the head of his cock to her pussy. She was hot and wet.

"You're more than ready, Emma," he said, and glided right into her.

Chapter Eleven

While he pumped his cock in-and-out of her, she gasped and moaned, clutched at him, kissed him, wrapped her legs around him, begging him not to stop, to go at her harder and harder . . .

He ducked his head, took her nipples into his mouth and bit them as she grabbed his head and clutched it to her. All the while their hips kept moving. Suddenly she pushed at him, and he knew what she wanted. He rolled over so that she was now on top.

She became more active, then, using all her energy to bounce up and down on him, causing her full breasts to jump and jiggle in front of him.

Obviously, Emma had gotten over her case of nerves. She was fully committing to making those memories. The smile on her face made that clear.

"Oh God!" she groaned aloud. "Goddamn, Gunsmith. If you can shoot as good as you do this—"

"Never mind that," he said. "Just keep going."

She pressed her hands down onto his abdomen, pushing herself up and coming down on him even harder, then twisting.

"Goddamn!" he said, through clenched teeth. He was trying to last long enough for Emma to get all the memories she wanted. Suddenly, she began to tremble uncontrollably, bounce even more vigorously, and then collapsed on top of him—just as he exploded inside of her . . .

***

"Memories?" he asked her, as he got dressed.

"Tons!" she said, happily. "How about you?"

"Oh yes," he said, "I'm going to remember Emma Deane, from Hannibal."

"Good." She rolled over on the bed so she was lying on her stomach. "Come by my café tomorrow. Bring Mr. Verne."

"All right."

"I'll feed you both and I won't charge you."

"No," Clint said, "we'll pay. You don't owe me anything."

She frowned.

"Did I offend you?"

"No," he said. "You just don't have to feed me for free because of this."

"All right," she said. "But I will see you tomorrow?"

"Probably," Clint said. "Sam wants to show Verne around, so I suppose we'll be needing supper later in the day."

"That's good," she said. "My place is the best place to have supper."

"I can believe that."

She quickly got off the bed as he strapped on his gun, padded naked to him, put her arms around his neck and kissed him.

"Thanks for walking me home."

"You're very welcome."

"Let me get my robe and I'll see you to the door."

"I'll find my way," Clint said. "Good-night, Emma."

"I enjoyed myself!" she called out to him.

"Charmed," he replied.

He left before she could say anything else.

Chapter Twelve

Clint woke the next morning to the smell of coffee. When he came downstairs, he saw Clemens and Jules Verne sitting at the dining room table, with cups in front of them.

"Coffee's in the kitchen," Clemens said.

"You made it?"

"I do know how to make coffee, Clint," Clemens said.

"How about bacon-and-eggs?"

"No."

"Do you have any?"

"I believe so."

"Then I'll make it," Clint said.

Clemens smiled.

"We were hoping you would."

Clint went into the kitchen, came back out a half hour later with three plates of bacon-and-eggs. He put them on the table, went back to the kitchen for the coffee pot, brought it out and poured all their cups full. Then he sat and started to eat.

"You got back late last night," Clemens said.

"I did," Clint said.

Clemens and Verne exchanged a look.

"Zee young lady is very lovely," Verne said.

"Yes, she is," Clint said. "What's your point, Jules?"

"I think his point is," Clemens said, "will she ever cook for me again."

"The answer's yes," Clint said. "In fact, she wants to cook for us today, at her café."

"Excellent!" Verne said. "I would love to have zee young lady cook for us again."

"Good!' Clemens snapped. "We'll eat there tonight. "But . . ." he looked at Clint. ". . . I have to say these eggs and bacon are great. Where'd you learn to cook like this?"

"On the trail."

"You eat like zees on zee trail?" Verne asked.

"Sometimes," Clint said. "Other times it's just beans or, if it's a cold camp, just some beef jerky."

"Fascinating!" Verne said. "Zees are things you could show me if you take me west."

"Yes," Clemens said, "we've been discussin' that."

"Have you, now?"

"Indeed," Clemens said. "I think it's a marvelous idea to show an esteemed visitor to our country as much of it as we can."

"We?"

"Well," Clemens said, "I'm gonna show him Hannibal. It's only fair that you show him the part of the country you know."

"I agree," Verne said. "Is zere anymore bacon?"

***

Since Clemens wanted to show Jules Verne his Hannibal, Clint decided to let the two of them go off by themselves, without him.

"Jules is waitin' for me on the porch," Clemens said. "Give it some thought, Clint. He's determined to see the West. If he goes by himself—"

"I get it," Clint said. "I'll give it some thought."

"Good," Clemens said. "We'll see you back here to go to Emma's for supper."

"Fine."

"What are you gonna do?"

"I'm going to sit on your porch," Clint said, "and think."

Clemens smiled. "Think long and hard."

Clemens left. Clint poured himself another cup of coffee, waited long enough for the two authors to get far enough away from the house, and then went out to sit.

***

Completely relaxed on the porch—but, of course, still alert for possible danger—Clint gave the matter of taking Jules Verne west a lot of thought. He finally realized he would agree for the same reason he had agreed to take Libbie Custer west to research her book about her husband. What if they went and something happened to them? Clint would feel guilty, because he'd been given the opportunity to keep them safe.

And he reminded himself again that with Libbie Custer, he had to deal with her shady publisher. This time around it was just Jules Verne, himself. Idly, he wondered if Sam Clemens was going to want to come with them, or if he had some "Mark Twain" business to take care of?

Clint found himself in the kitchen, cleaning the mess he had made preparing breakfast. This hadn't been the way he thought he'd be spending his day. When he was done, he decided to take a walk through downtown Hannibal, and down by the Mississippi River.

When he returned the two authors still were not home, so he grabbed his copy of Verne's book that he had been reading and picked up where he'd left off with Captain Nemo.

Chapter Thirteen

Clint was still on the porch, reading 20,000 Leagues when Clemens and Verne returned.

"Good God," Clemens barked, as they came up the walk, "have you been there all day?"

"I've been up-and-down," Clint said. "How did you fellas do?"

"I have seen many Hannibal wonders," Jules Verne said, enthusiastically. "Including Miss Becky Thatcher's house."

"That's great," Clint said.

"Still followin' Captain Nemo, huh?" Clemens asked.

"I'm almost finished," Clint said. "He's a fascinating character."

"Yes, he is," Clemens said.

"I thank you both," Verne said, with a short bow.

As he stepped up onto the porch his limp seemed to Clint to be pronounced.

"Have a seat, Jules," Clint said. "Give that leg a rest."

"I am fine," Verne lied.

"How about we apply some bourbon to that leg?" Clemens asked.

"Zat sounds like an excellent idea!" Verne said.

"I'll get it."

Verne sat in the wicker chair next to Clint's.

"Did he wear you out?" Clint asked.

"I am fine, I assure you," Verne said. "This leg always looks worse zen it feels."

Clemens came out with two glasses of bourbon, knowing that Clint wouldn't be interested. He handed one to Verne, then sat on Clint's other side.

"Walkin' around Hannibal sure works up a man's appetite," Clemens said. "I'm glad Emma suggested we go to her place and eat."

"She was going to feed us for free, but I insisted that we pay her."

"Of course!" Clemens said. "After all, I paid her for last night, too. The girl needs to make a livin'."

"Zat is very true," Verne said, lifting his glass.

"I think we just need to clean up and then we can take your buggy over to the café, instead of walkin' on that leg."

"I will not argue."

Clint had unhitched the horse the night before and put it and Eclipse in a small shed behind Clemens' house.

"I'll get it hitched up," he said, standing. "You fellas enjoy your bourbon."

Clint went around behind the house, hitched the horse to the buggy and walked him around to the front. Then he tied him to the hitching post and rejoined the two writers on the porch.

"Are we ready?" Clint asked.

Verne drained his glass and said, "I am ready."

"Let me take these glasses inside," Clemens said. "Clint? The book?"

"Oh, sure, thanks." Clint handed Clemens his copy of 20,000 Leagues.

When Clemens came back out, he said, "Off to Emma's. She's gonna be crowded, but if she's expectin' us, she'll save a table."

They stepped down off the porch and headed for the buggy.

***

The buggy was a two-seater, but Clemens happily sat on the back, where luggage usually went, and waved at his neighbors as they drove by.

Clint stopped the buggy in front of Emma's little café, which had her name right above the door: EMMA'S. Clemens nimbly dropped to the ground, while Verne was slower, but still managed to get himself down on his own, which Clint knew by now was important to the man.

They entered the café and saw that it was, indeed, crowded. Almost every table was taken. But Emma came running up to them with a big smile on her face.

"You came!"

"I said we would," Clint said, "and when I told these gents you invited us, they insisted."

"I saved your table, Sam," she said.

"Thank you, my dear."

They followed her to a table in the back. As opposed to the red-and-white checkerboard tablecloths on the other tables, this one was covered by an all-white cloth.

"I hate those checkerboard things," Clemens said to Clint and Verne.

They sat, Verne being the one who ended up with his back to the room. Emma promised to return with coffee for all of them.

"Zis is charming," Verne said, looking around. "And it seems very popular."

"Like I told you," Clemens said, "best food in town."

"She proved that last night," Clint said. He didn't add what else she had proved.

Emma came over with coffee and then asked the three men what they wanted to eat.

"Or do you want it to be a surprise?" she asked.

The three exchanged a look, and then Clemens said, "Okay, surprise us."

Chapter Fourteen

She brought them steak dinners, and Clint had to admit it was the best he'd ever had—and he ate steak, a lot. Also, the surrounding vegetables—potatoes, carrots, and broccoli—were perfectly prepared.

"Zees is incredible," Jules Verne said, halfway through the meal.

"Yes, it is," Clemens said.

"Someone should write about zee girl," Verne said.

"Write about her?" Clint asked. "You mean, like, in a newspaper."

"No," Verne said, "I mean in a story, or a book."

"You mean, make her a character," Clemens said.

"Yes."

"Why?" Clint asked.

"She is special," Verne said.

"Why don't you do it?" Clint asked.

"No one in France would believe it," Verne said. "We have beautiful women, but not special ones."

"Wow," Clemens said. "I wouldn't expect you to say that."

"I have been surprised at how forthright American women are," Verne said. "I like it."

"Well," Clint said, "I can't complain."

Clemens scratched his cheek thoughtfully.

"I do write about Hannibal," he commented. "Why not add Emma?"

"Wonderful!"

"Just don't tell 'er," Clemens said. "She'll probably wanna tell me how to do it. I don't mind folks advising me about what to write, but I can't stand when they try to tell me how to write."

"On that I must agree," Verne said.

He and Clemens clinked glasses, and then went back to eating.

***

Folks came and went while Clint, Clemens and Jules Verne ate their supper. Many of them were families.

After Emma had cleared the table of the remains she said, "Dessert?"

"What did you have in mind?" Clemens asked.

"Another surprise."

"The first one went well," Clint said, "so sure, surprise us again."

She brought them each something she called sticky toffee pudding.

"*Mon Dieu,*" Jules Verne declared after one bite. "*Etonner*!"

"Come again?" Clemens asked.

"Amazing," Verne said, "simply amazing flavor."

"I have to agree there," Clint said, "although it's a little sweet for my taste."

"I do not mind," the French author said. "I have zee—how do you say it—*dent sucrée*. Zee sweet tooth?"

"I kinda got one of those, myself," Clemens said.

They washed the pudding down with more coffee, and by the time they were done the café was fairly empty. When Emma accepted payment from her final customers of the night, she walked over to their table.

"I'll bet you gents would like some bourbon to top everything off."

"*Exactement!*" Verne said, in agreement.

"You bet," Clemens agreed.

"I'd rather have a beer," Clint said.

"Comin' up!" she said, and hurried back to the kitchen. When she came out, she had a tray bearing four drinks—three bourbons and one beer.

"I hope you don't mind if I join you," she said.

"Please do," Clint said, and pulled over another chair.

Chapter Fifteen

After dessert Emma said she had some cleaning up to do before she could leave.

"Do you want Clint to stay and walk you home?" Clemens asked.

"No," she said, "not tonight. I'll be fine."

"Are you sure?" Verne asked.

"Yes," she said, not looking at Clint, "I'm sure."

"All right then," Clemens said. "Good-night."

The three men started walking back to Sam Clemens' house.

***

"I'm gonna smoke a pipe on the porch," Clemens said.

"I zink I will go to sleep," Verne said. "I will see you both in the morning."

"Good-night," Clint said.

As Verne went inside, Clemens asked Clint, "Sit with me?"

"Sure."

They both sat and Clemens got his pipe going.

"Have you decided?" he asked.

"Decided what?"

"Come on, Clint, you know what I mean," Clemens scolded him. "Are you gonna take our friend, Verne, west with you?"

"I've pretty much decided yes, but—"

"Excellent!"

"—*but*," Clint went on, "I have to see if he can ride. We'll make better time if we don't have to take a buggy."

"What's the rush?"

"No rush," Clint said, "it's just easier to get around on horseback. We won't have to stick to established roads."

"That makes sense," Clemens said. "You know, the goddamned government should've sent somebody to escort him around."

"We don't know how things went for him in D.C.," Clint said.

"If one of us knew he was comin' ahead of time we coulda used a contact or two to get him taken care of."

"You really think the government would've been impressed with him?"

"He's a well-known gent from another country," Clemens said. "When I went to Canada, they treated me like a king."

"Too late now," Clint said. "I'll just have to do my best to make him feel like a king."

"I think you'll have to beat what Emma and I did here in Hannibal," Clemens said, proudly.

"You're probably right." Clint stood. "I'm going to turn in, then Jules and I can get an early start tomorrow after breakfast."

"Good plan."

"I don't suppose you'd want to come west with us?" Clint asked.

"Naw," Clemens said, "I got some appointments. I'll be leavin' Hannibal myself day after tomorrow to head back East."

"I thought that might be the case," Clint said, "but I just wanted to ask. Good-night, Sam."

"'night, Clint."

***

In the morning Clint came down, and had the feeling that Clemens might have fallen asleep on the porch. He looked tired, and seemed to be dressed in the same clothes. However, he had made coffee, and they all sat at the dining room table and drank it with some leftover biscuits they slathered with butter.

After Clint had hitched the horse to the buggy Clemens walked out onto the porch with them. The two authors shook hands warmly.

"It was a pleasure to have ya here, Jules."

"I will try to treat you as well, *mon ami*, if you come to see me in France," Verne promised.

"I'll holdja to that." Clemens turned and shook hands with Clint. "See ya again soon, my friend."

"Give 'em hell, Mr. Twain."

He and Verne climbed back aboard the buggy and headed for St. Louis.

Chapter Sixteen

During the buggy ride from Hannibal to St. Louis Verne assured Clint that yes, indeed—or *oui*—he could certainly ride a horse. Clint decided they would head west from St. Louis on a train, and when they reached Council Bluffs, Iowa, he would then buy a horse for Verne to ride.

They checked back into the same hotel Clint had been in before they left and had supper in the dining room. Over the meal Verne talked about Sam Clemens and what a fascinating and generous man he was.

After supper they went to the lobby and Verne said, “Do not let me keep you, Clint. I know you probably want to go to a saloon to gamble and drink.”

“What?”

“Is that not what you do in the West?” Verne asked. “Gamble and drink?”

“There are other things to do, Jules,” Clint said. “For instance, I’m going to my room and finish your book, so I can start the next one. When I’m done with Captain Nemo, I’m looking forward to going to the center of the earth.”

“I apologize, *mon ami*,” Verne said. “I did not mean to insult you.”

"You didn't insult me," Clint assured him. "I realize all you have as reference for things you've heard or read. I just wish you hadn't read those dime novels that book dealer gave you."

"*Mon ami,*" Verne said, again, "I have already learned that the Gunsmith in those books is not you."

"Well, that's good to hear."

"The author who wrote those books should be sued," Verne went on.

"That won't be necessary," Clint said. "I haven't even seen them in a very long time. They mean nothing to me."

"That is good," Verne said. "Still, if it was me, I would sue zem."

"Then you care more about what people think of you than I do."

"Of course," Verne said. "I need people to like and respect me so zat zey will buy my books."

"I understand," Clint said. "Why don't we both go to our rooms and get some rest?"

"Agreed," Verne said. "I have one of Mark Twain's books to read."

"And I have another of yours to start."

"Journey?" Verne asked.

"Yes."

They started to walk together.

"Zat is a good one," Verne said.

"Jules," Clint said, "I'll take you west, show you some of the famous places, maybe even introduce you to some of the people."

"That is wonderful."

"But I want something from you."

"What would zat be?"

"I want to learn why you do what you do."

"I write because I must," Verne said. "I do not have a choice."

"I get that," Clint said. "I'm interested in why you write what you write."

"Ah, you mean why do I write about people going to zee center of zee earth, or under za sea."

"Yes."

"Zen *oui*," Verne said, "we will talk about it."

"Good," Clint said.

They walked to their doors, which were across from each other.

"Good-night, Clint," Verne said.

"Good-night, Jules. Tomorrow, we go West."

Chapter Seventeen

In the morning Clint discussed with Jules Verne what the man expected to see when going west.

"Cowboys," Verne said, "Indians, train robbers and a deputy sheriff—"

"Okay," Clint said. "You can see all of that right here in Missouri."

"There are Indians in Missouri?"

"There are Indians everywhere," Clint said.

"I would like to see the Indians who are the most savage," Verne said.

"No," Clint said, "trust me, you wouldn't."

***

Later that day Clint walked Eclipse onto the stock car of the train they would be taking from St. Louis to Des Moines, Iowa. After that he joined Jules Verne in the passenger car, allowing the French author to sit by the window.

"All right," Clint said, as the train started, "here we go."

***

Further toward the back of the passenger car two men sat with their heads together.

"Are you sure it's him?" Sam Partridge asked.

"Yeah, I'm sure," Dan Train said. "I saw him in Abilene, once. It's him."

"Great," Partridge said, "how the hell are we gonna rob a train that has the Gunsmith on it?"

"I think the question is," Train said, "how do we not rob a train that has the Gunsmith on it?"

"What?"

"If this gets out," Train said, "we'll be famous."

"But . . . we'd have to go up against him."

"I have an idea."

"What?"

"It looks like he's travelin' with a friend," Train said. "An old guy."

"I saw him. So?"

"So we grab him first," Train said. "After that, the Gunsmith is ours. And so is everythin' on this train that's worth anythin'."

"That sounds good, I guess," his partner said.

"Look, don't worry about a thing," Train said. "Don't I always come up with a plan?"

Partridge didn't reply, and Train didn't seem to notice.

***

Clint and Verne went to the dining car. He remembered the times with Libbie Custer recently, and started to wish he had put Verne on a horse right from St. Louis.

"So how much riding have you done?" Clint asked.

Verne hesitated, then said, "Some."

"When?"

"When I was younger."

"How much younger?"

"Would you gents care to order?" a waiter asked.

"Yes, we would," Verne said, taking the opportunity not to answer Clint's question. "I will have zee roasted chicken."

"Sir?" the waiter asked, looking at Clint.

"I'll just have the same."

"And to drink?"

"Two beers," Clint said.

"Comin' up, sir."

"Do you want to answer my question about riding?" Clint asked, as the waiter walked away.

"I rode as a young man," Jules Verne said. "alzough I have not ridden for a while, I believe I will be fine."

"All right," Clint said. "When we get to Des Moines we'll buy you a horse."

"A gentle, but strong, horse," Verne suggested.

"That sounds right," Clint said.

***

Back in the passenger car they both took out the books they were going to read on the trip—Clint *Journey to The Center of the Earth.* Verne had Twain's *A Connecticut Yankee in King Arthur's Court.*

"Before we start reading," Clint said, "tell me why you write the books you write."

"I zink we should save zat for the nights on zee trail," Verne said.

"All right, then," Clint said. "Let's split the difference."

"I am sorry," Verne said. "What does zis mean, split zee difference."

"It means you don't have to tell me why you write what you write," Clint said, "but you can tell me why you wrote this particular book."

Verne gave that some thought, then said, "Fine, we will split zee difference."

Chapter Eighteen

"Excuse me."

Clint looked up from his book, saw a tall, grey-haired man in a conductor's uniform and hat staring down at him.

"Yes?"

"Are you Clint Adams?"

"Yes, I am."

"I'm sorry to bother you," the man said, "I'm the conductor, George Starr, and I believe I have a problem you could help me with."

Now Verne looked up from his book, wanting to hear what the man's request was going to be.

"I think there are two men on the train who are planning to rob it."

"Don't you have a security man on board?"

"Usually, we do," Starr said, "but not this trip. He got sick and there was no time to replace him."

"What makes you think they're going to rob the train?" Clint asked.

"I've been on this job for many years," he said. "I just . . . they don't feel right."

Clint could respect that feeling from someone who had been working his job a long time. He also had feelings about people, which were usually right.

But . . .

“What do you want me to do about it?”

“Keep an eye on ’em,” Starr said. “Make sure they don’t rob the train. Or . . .”

“Or?” Verne said. “Stop zem now.”

Clint looked at Verne, then back at the conductor.

“You could stop them,” he said, “or better yet, make them get off the train.”

“Because you suspect they *might* rob the train?” Clint asked. “Can you do that?”

“I’m responsible for all the passengers on this train,” Starr said. “If I think someone is a danger to them, I can put them off.”

“Then do it,” Clint said. “Just put them off.”

Starr hesitated, looked around at the other passengers. The ones closest to Clint and Verne were dozing.

“I can’t do it alone,” Starr said, lowering his voice. “Can you do it with me?”

“Where are they?”

“In the next car,” Starr said.

“Is it full?”

“Yes.”

"If I do this," Clint said, "we'll need to confront them somewhere away from the other passengers."

"To keep anyone from getting hurt?" Verne asked.

Clint looked at him.

"To keep anyone from being used as a hostage."

"Oh."

Clint looked at Starr.

"I tell you what," he said to the conductor. "I'll take a look at these fellas and tell you what I think."

"And if you agree they're trouble?"

"Then we'll do something about it," Clint said, "together."

"Okay. Let's go."

"No," Clint said, standing up, "you stay here. I want to see if I can pick them out."

"All right," Starr agreed.

Clint looked at Verne.

"You stay here, too," he said. "Talk with the nice man."

"As you wish."

Clint walked down the center aisle, heading for the other passenger car. As he did so he heard Verne behind him, saying, "Hello, I am Jules Verne."

"Really?" Starr asked. "The Captain Nemo writer?"

***

As he entered the second car not many of the passengers looked up at him. They were busy staring out the window, reading, deep in conversation, or dozing. Starr had said the two suspicious men were toward the back.

He started walking slowly, trying not to be obvious about what he was doing. As he looked people over, several glanced up at him and either looked away immediately, or smiled, or nodded.

There were several seats with two men sitting together. But in each case one of the men didn't match Starr's description.

But when he got a good look at the two in the back, he knew it was them. Now all he had to decide was if they had train robbery in mind.

Both men not only didn't look at him as he went by, but they diverted their eyes. They were feeling guilty about something.

He could have kept walking, left the car, waited a few minutes and then returned, but there was also the possibility they wouldn't be there. They might run into the next passenger car, threaten some people, or simply jump off the train. Jumping wasn't a problem, but hurting people was.

Clint stopped and looked down at them.

"You boys have to come with me."

Chapter Nineteen

Both men stared up at him, and he knew what they were thinking.

"It wouldn't be a good idea to resist," he said.

"We ain't done nothin'," one of them said.

"Yet," Clint said, "and we're not willing to wait until you do."

"We?"

"The conductor."

One of the men looked at the other.

"I told you he was looking at us funny."

"So let's stand up very slowly, and the first one who goes for their gun gets a bullet."

"What if one of us outdraws you?" one asked.

"That's not likely. Come on."

Slowly, they stood up.

"Now step out into the aisle and start walking to the other car."

"Aren't you gonna take our guns?" one asked.

"No," Clint said, "you're going to need them."

"For what?"

"You'll see. Keep moving."

They got to the end of the car, opened the door and stepped outside. As one of the men reached for the door to the next car, Clint stopped him.

"No, no," Clint said, "you've come as far as you're going go."

"Whataya mean?"

"I mean, you two jump."

"Off the train?"

"That's right."

"But . . . we'll get killed."

"No you won't," Clint said. "Just bend your knees when you land, and roll. You'll be fine."

"But . . . why are you doin' this?"

"Just a precaution," Clint said. "You either jump, or get a bullet."

The two men moved out to the edge of the platform. One jumped, and then the other. Clint went back inside without checking to see if they had tucked and rolled.

***

"Whataya mean, it's done?" the conductor asked.

"Done," Clint said, sitting back down next to Verne.

"They're gone?"

"They are."

"How?"

"They decided to leave the train."

The conductor's eyes went wide.

"You kicked them off the train?"

"Let's say they decided to jump rather than face the other options."

"*Pardon*," Verne said. "You made them jump off the train?"

"Oh," Clint said, "I made sure we were passing a nice, grassy section. And I told them how to bend their knees and roll."

"*Manifique*!" Verne said.

"Wait—"

"Go have a look," Clint said. "I think your train will be safe, now."

"Oh, yeah," Starr said, "right. I'll, uh, go and look. Thank you."

"Uh-huh."

As the conductor headed back up the aisle Verne leaned over.

"Did you really make zee men jump off the train?"

"Yes, I did."

"I wish I could haf seen zat!" he said, his eyes shining.

"Well . . . maybe next time," Clint said.

***

The conductor, Starr, went into the other car, closed the door, kept his back to it, looked around, then reached behind him, opened the door, and stepped out. He turned and rushed back into Clint's car.

***

"What the hell are you talking about?" Clint asked.

"They're still there," Starr said. "The two men I was telling you about. They're still sitting in the other car."

"That can't be," Clint said.

"Mr. Adams," Starr said, "I'm afraid you kicked the wrong two men off the train."

Clint stared at the man. If that was true, then he had made two innocent men jump off a moving train.

"No," he said.

"Whataya mean, no?" Starr asked. "You didn't throw them off the train?"

"I mean they weren't innocent," Clint said. "They acted real guilty about something."

"So that justifies throwing them off the train?" Starr asked.

"Show me the two men you were talking about," Clint said.

Chapter Twenty

"Those two."

Clint saw the two men the conductor meant. He tried to put aside the picture in his mind of the other two men jumping off the train. He only hoped whatever it was they *were* guilty of, it was worth the bumps and bruises.

But he put them aside and looked at these two. The others had been dressed as cowhands, regular trail clothes. These two were dressed for travel, but they also wore guns on their hips.

The two men were not looking at Clint or Starr. One was reading a newspaper, while the other dozed with his arms folded across his chest.

"Do you want to make them jump off the train now?" Starr asked.

"No!" Clint said. "Right now let's just leave them alone."

"But . . . what if they try—"

"Let's just watch them for a few minutes, and then see what they do."

The conductor nodded.

"Okay."

***

"They're gone," Partridge said, opening his eyes and unfolding his arms.

"They'll be back," Train said, without looking up from the newspaper he was reading.

"What's so interestin' in the paper?" Partridge asked. "Ain't you worried about the Gunsmith anymore?"

"Not really."

"You mean you think we can go ahead and rob the train?" Partridge asked, lowering his voice.

"No," Train said, "I mean I don't think we'll have to."

"Why not?"

Train held the newspaper out so Partridge could see what he was reading . . .

***

"I wouldn't have minded," Starr said, "if you'd made those two jump off the train."

They were back in the other passenger car.

"Forget that," Clint said. "What I did was a mistake. I tell you what. I'll watch those two and make sure they don't rob the train."

"The rest of the way to Des Moines?" Starr asked.

"Yes," Clint said, "the rest of the way."

That made the conductor very happy.

***

Clint decided to leave Jules Verne seated in the first car while he moved to the second. He found a single seat with no one else around it and settled in. From there he could see the two men who worried the conductor. It didn't seem that they had moved, one reading, the other dozing. Then he noticed something. They had switched. It was the other who was now reading, and the other dozing.

He watched them closely.

***

The train pulled into the station in Des Moines without incident. The two men seemed satisfied to remain in their seats, and the conductor was happy with that.

Clint went into the other car to join Jules Verne.

"I'm going to the stock car to collect Eclipse," he told the author. "Just wait for me on the platform."

"As you wish."

On the way to the stock car he encountered the conductor.

"Everything okay?" he asked.

"It seems to be," Starr said. "Those men got off, and I don't think they're getting back on, so I thank you for your help, Mr. Adams."

"Sure." Clint still hadn't quite come to terms with the fact he had forced the wrong two men to jump off the train.

"Would you like me to send someone to bring you your horse?" Starr asked.

"No, I'll get him myself. Thanks."

Clint walked back to the stock car, where he was able to board, saddle Eclipse, and then walk him off with no problem.

He walked the Darley to a point at the end of the platform, then went back to where he had told Jules Verne to wait, only the man wasn't there.

He checked both ends of the platform, but didn't see him. That was when he went looking for Starr, the conductor, again.

"Have you seen Mr. Verne?" he asked him. "I had him waiting for me on the platform while I got my horse."

"No, haven't seen him."

"Could you ask around for me?"

"Sure."

While the conductor went to talk to some of the clerks in the station, Clint got back on the train. He walked through both passenger cars, and when he got to the seat the two men had been occupying, he saw the newspaper they had been reading. When he picked it up and saw what page it was folded to, he knew what had happened.

Chapter Twenty-One

Clint found the conductor, Starr, on the platform.

"I'm afraid I have bad news," Starr said.

"I know," Clint handed him the newspaper.

"What's this?"

"The paper your two men were reading."

Starr looked down at the copy of the *St. Louis Post-Dispatch*, Clint handed him, saw Jules Verne's face and name prominently displayed.

"I don't—"

"Once they saw this, they changed their plan," Clint said.

"One of the clerks saw them walking away with Mr. Verne between them," Starr said.

"Right," Clint said, "while I was getting my horse, they snatched him off the platform."

"But why?"

"Why else?" Clint asked. "He's an internationally known author. They're going to hold him for ransom."

"Ransom to be paid by who?" Starr asked.

"Whoever," Clint said. "His government, our government."

"And how do they expect to contact those governments?" Starr asked.

"Probably through me."

"So what will you do?"

"Get a hotel room," Clint said, "and wait."

He was also going to send a telegram to Washington D.C.

***

Clint got a room at the nearest decent hotel to the train station. It was called The Blossom House, and wouldn't have normally been his choice. The lobby was decorated with blossom wallpaper.

He checked in, got his key and asked the clerk, "Where's the nearest telegraph office?"

"Just down the street, sir," the man said.

"And a livery?"

"Same direction," the clerk said. "You should come to the telegraph office, first."

"Thanks."

He left and walked Eclipse down the street, with people turning to look. He hoped they were just looking at the Darley, and that word hadn't gone around that he was in town.

When he came to the telegraph office he left Eclipse outside, his reins hanging to the ground. He pitied anyone who tried to make him move.

Inside he sat and tried to figure out how to word his telegram, and who to send it to. He had to make it clear in as few words as possible that he had taken Jules Verne west, and the French author had then been kidnapped. His fault, pure and simple. He wasn't looking forward to telling anyone that. In the end he decided to send the missive to his friend, Jim West, a Secret Service Agent. Jim could then direct it to the right people.

He wrote it, got it sent off, and then continued on to the livery. He accepted the usual admiration from the hostler, got the Darley taken care of, then took his saddle-bags and rifle back to his hotel with him.

***

In his room he sat with Verne's *Journey to the Bottom of the Sea* in his hands. He was thinking about opening it when there was a knock at his door. He grabbed his gun from the gunbelt hanging on the bedpost and went to answer it.

"Who is it?"

"It's George Starr," a man's voice said, and then added, "the conductor from the train."

Clint opened the door a crack and peered out at the man, standing there alone. He opened it wider.

"What can I do for you?"

"It's what I can do for you, Mr. Adams," the conductor said. "I feel that Mr. Verne's kidnapping is partially my fault."

"Come on in," Clint said. He stepped back, allowed the man to enter, then closed the door and turned to him. "How do you figure?"

"Maybe if I hadn't asked you to help me with those two men, it wouldn't have happened."

"They still would have read the paper," Clint said. "Recognized Verne."

"Yes, but they might have gone ahead and tried to rob the train before that."

"So what can you do?"

"I've already done it." He handed Clint a piece of paper.

"What's this?"

"Their names," Starr said. "That is, the names they bought the tickets under. I realize it's probably not their real names, if they were planning to rob the train, but it's something."

"They just might've been dumb enough to buy the tickets under their real names," Clint said. "Thank you, George."

"Sure thing," Starr said. "I wish I could do more."

"I thought you woul've been gone today," Clint said.

"I'm catching a train back in the other direction, leaving tomorrow afternoon," Starr said.

"Well, thank you for this."

Starr nodded and Clint let him out. He looked at the names on the piece of paper: Sam Partridge and Dan Train. He shook his head. Train. Great name for a train robber.

Chapter Twenty-Two

Clint went down for breakfast the next day. He was itching to do more, but he didn't have idea one about where to start looking for Jules Verne. So he decided to eat breakfast, and then take his problem to the local law.

He found the sheriff's office, but it was across the street from a large building that housed a more modern police department. The question was, which one would be more helpful?

He finally decided he had more faith in old line lawmen then any new, modern police department. He entered the sheriff's office. A middle-aged man wearing a badge almost ran right into him, stopped short.

"You just caught me," the lawman said, putting on his hat "I was on my way out."

"This won't take long."

The lawman took off his hat.

"Okay, then, what's on your mind?" the lawman said. "I'm Sheriff Cal Lariman, by the way."

"Clint Adams."

Lariman stared at Clint for a moment, then backed toward his desk.

"I think I gotta sit down for this." He moved around the desk and lowered himself into his chair. "Why don't you take a chair and tell me what the Gunsmith is doing in Des Moines?"

"Actually, I was just passing through, but circumstances have changed."

"Circumstances being . . .?"

"Kidnapping."

"Who was kidnapped?"

"Jules Verne."

The sheriff looked confused.

"And who, or what, is a . . . Jules Verne?"

"He's a French writer visiting the United States," Clint said. "He and I were traveling on the train, and when we got here he was taken."

"By who?"

"As far as I know, two men, one named Partridge and the other Train."

"Wait, he was kidnapped off the train by a man named Train?"

"That's right."

"Okay," Lariman said, holding his hand up, "just wanted to make sure I had that right. Why have you come to me?"

"I need to find those two men," Clint said. "I thought I'd describe them to you, see if you knew them. That is, if you didn't recognize their names."

"I don't. Let's hear the descriptions."

Clint described the two men in turn, but he didn't know which one was Partridge and which one was Train.

"Those descriptions could match anybody," Lariman said. "I think we better go across the street."

"Why?"

Because I don't have any deputies," Lariman said. "We can give the descriptions to the department across the street, and they can search all over town."

"Okay," Clint said. "Sounds good."

Lariman stood up and put his hat back on.

"So this Verne, he's famous?"

"He's as famous in France as Mark Twain is in the United States," Clint said.

"Really?" Lariman said, as they headed for the door. "Who's Mark Twain?"

***

Lariman walked Clint across the street and into the building that housed the Des Moines Police Department.

"Sheriff," the policeman on the front desk greeted, "can I help you?"

"I need to see your chief," Lariman said. "Right away."

"And who's this?" the man asked.

"Clint Adams," Lariman said. "The Gunsmith. He has a problem we need to help him with."

"The Gunsmith needs us?" the policeman asked.

"In a big way," Clint said.

"Okay, then," the man said, "follow me."

He led them deeper into the building and down a hall to an open door that he knocked on.

"Chief? Sheriff Lariman's here for you."

"Send 'im in," a male voice said.

"You can go in," the policeman said, stepping aside.

"Thank you," the sheriff said.

Clint followed Lariman into the room. A large, florid-faced man stood behind his desk, smiling. He frowned when he saw Clint.

"What can I do for you, Sheriff?"

"Not me," Lariman said. "This is Clint Adams. He has a problem he needs help with."

"Mr. Adams?" the man said. "I'm Chief Whitlock. What can I help you with?"

"First," Clint said, "do you know who Jules Verne is?"

"Yes," the chief said. "Why is that important?"

"It'll just make things easier."

Chapter Twenty-Three

Partridge came in the room and looked at Dan Train.

"Did you know who this guy was when you read the story in the newspaper?" he asked.

"No," Train said. "I never heard of him before that."

"But you think this is a good idea?" Partridge asked.

"Yeah, I do," Train said. "He's from another country and they ain't gonna want somethin' to happen to him while he's here."

"We coulda got valuables off the train passengers," Partridge said.

"We would've got some," Train said, "if our other two partners hadn't disappeared. And if Clint Adams didn't stop us. But this way we're gonna get more. A helluva lot more."

"From Adams?"

"No," Train said, standing up and facing his partner, "through Adams."

"So when are we gonna do that?" Partridge asked.

"First," Train said, "we're gonna get Verne out of Des Moines."

"Where are we goin'?"

"I haven't decided yet," Train said. "but we're gonna get out of Des Moines."

"And when are we doin' that?" Partridge asked.

"I've got that figured," Train said. "We'll leave tomorrow."

"You know Adams is gonna be all over the streets, lookin' for this guy," Partridge said. "How do we slip outta town without him seein' us?"

"Don't worry," Train said, tapping his forehead, "I got that figured, too."

***

"That's quite a story," Chief Whitlock said.

Clint had left off the part about having made two men jump off the train, innocent or not. He didn't think it was pertinent.

He and the sheriff had taken seats in front of the chief's desk, while the large man had seated himself in his chair to listen.

"Meaning?" Clint asked.

"Have you gotten a ransom demand yet?"

"No."

"Then how do you know the man was kidnapped?"

"He was seen walking off the platform with two other men," Clint said.

"Maybe he had made friends with them on the train," Whitlock suggested.

"That's doubtful. I was with him on the train."

"The entire time?"

"Except for when I was watching Train and Partridge," Clint admitted.

"Ah, the alleged kidnappers?" Whitlock said.

"Alleged?"

"Yes," the chief said, "it's a word we use when there's no proof about an accusation."

"This is not just an accusation, Chief," Clint said. "This is a fact."

"A fact, Mr. Adams," the chief said, "is something you can prove. Can you prove this? And I mean, to the satisfaction of the law."

Clint hesitated a moment, looked at the sheriff, and said, "I suppose not."

"Maybe the sheriff can help you," the chief said, "but we can't. Not until we know there's been a crime."

"Then why don't we just say I'm trying to stop a kidnapping?" Clint suggested.

"Then I wish you luck." The chief stood. "Other than that, there's nothing I can do right now." He looked at Lariman. "Sheriff?"

Lariman stood.

"Chief," he said.

The sheriff turned to leave. Clint hesitated, then followed him.

***

Outside the police station Clint stopped next to Sheriff Lariman.

"Did you expect that?"

"Well, I can't exactly say I did," the sheriff said. "But I can't say I'm surprised, either. The chief is a by-the-book guy."

"Well," Clint said, "I guess I'm going to have to search this town myself."

"Oh, I'll take a look around with you," the sheriff said. "I mean, I don't much mind stopping a kidnapping before it starts."

"Oh, it's started, all right," Clint said. "Just not according to that man."

"Des Moines has grown by leaps and bounds of late," Sheriff Lariman said, "it's gettin' bigger while we stand here and jaw."

"Then I guess we better get started," Clint said. "Just give me some idea of a route to take."

Lariman stepped off the boardwalk onto the street and Clint followed.

"Some areas probably aren't even worth lookin' at," Lariman told him. "At least, not until we look at some of the more likely ones." He put his hand on Clint's arm. "Why don't you start . . .

Chapter Twenty-Four

Thanks to the advice of Sheriff Lariman, Clint checked several hotels and rooming houses where Partridge and Train may have been holding Jules Verne. Along the way he also stopped into saloons with his descriptions of the two men, as well as Jules Verne.

When he returned to his hotel the desk clerk waved his telegram at him.

"Thanks," Clint said, accepting it.

He walked over to sit on a sofa in the lobby and unfolded the message. Jim West assured him that help was on the way. Clint only hoped it got there before he had to leave town.

He was about to rise to his feet when he saw Sheriff Lariman enter, so he stayed where he was and let the man approach him.

The lawman sat next to Clint, who asked, "Any luck?"

"No," Lariman said. "Nobody's seen anythin'—or, if they have, they're not sayin'. What about you? Come up with anythin'?"

"Nothing," Clint said, waving the telegram, "but I've been assured that help is coming."

"From where?"

"The government."

Lariman's eyebrows went up.

"Impressive," he said. "A federal marshal?"

"We'll know exactly who it is when they arrive," Clint said. "I just hope they get here in time."

"So what do you plan to do until then?"

"Just keep looking," Clint said.

"You're gonna have to stop for a meal, or a drink," the lawman said, getting to his feet, "let me recommend the Stockyard Steakhouse, down the street. Best steaks in town. I won't be there, but maybe I'll see you in the Red Roan Saloon later."

"Red Roan?"

"You'll see."

Sheriff Lariman left the lobby, and Clint went up to his room.

***

Clint's secret hope was that he'd find a ransom note slipped underneath his door. That wasn't to be the case. So he remained in his room for a while, hoping it would happen, then left to find the Stockyard Steakhouse.

***

The Stockyard Steakhouse was obviously a popular place, but the sheriff had apparently made sure they were watching for Clint Adams' arrival.

"Mr. Adams?" a man in a black suit asked, as he entered.

"That's right."

"This way, sir," the man said, "I have your table ready."

"Thank you."

The man took Clint to the back of the room, which suited him. The sheriff obviously knew he wouldn't want to sit anywhere near a window.

"A menu, sir?" the man asked, as Clint sat.

"Not necessary," Clint said. "I'll have a steak dinner with all the trimmings, and a beer."

"Good choice, sir," the man said. "Right away."

The man withdrew and Clint looked around. The tables and chairs all matched, a sign of money invested. Also, the tablecloths seemed to match the walls. In addition, the silverware on the table was heavy and ornate. He only hoped they had invested as much in their food.

The room was filled with people of all shapes and sizes, but what most of them had in common was that they were dressed well. None looked as if they had just come in off the trail. Clint had donned a clean shirt, but he still felt as if he was underdressed.

There were tables occupied by parties of twos and threes, others by families. There were only several with someone sitting alone, as Clint was. At one of them was a woman with pitch black hair, pale skin, red lips, wearing a dress that clung to her curves, and showed the upper slopes of her full breasts.

She was looking down, but seemed to sense she was being watched. When she raised her eyes and saw him she smiled, and he returned it with a nod.

He noticed there were other men also watching her, as she once again lowered her gaze. After a few moments she called the waiter over and said something to him, and the man turned to approach Clint.

"Sir, the lady would like to know if she can join you at your table," the waiter said.

"Did she say why?" Clint asked.

"Yes, sir," the waiter said. "She thinks maybe other men will stop watchin' her if she's sittin' with you."

"Well," Clint said, "you tell the lady I'd be happy to have her join me."

"Yes, sir!"

The waiter delivered the message and the lady stood, picked up her glass and walked over. Clint stood to hold her chair.

"Thank you so much," she said, as she sat. "My name's Diane Bellamy. I was considering leaving until I saw you looking over at me."

"Like all the other men here, I'm afraid," he said, as he sat back down.

"Not at all," she said. "Your look was kind, and admiring, while theirs were . . . well, considerably less than that."

"Glad to be of service, Ma'am."

Chapter Twenty-Five

Two waiters appeared, carrying their plates, and a mug of beer for Clint. They set the plates down, with steaks, potatoes, onions, carrots, as well as a basket of warm biscuits. By the time they left, the table was covered with food.

"This is a lot of food," he commented.

"You'll find I have a hearty appetite," she told him, smiling. "I suspect you do, too. I think we can handle all of this." we're about to see."

They dug into their steaks, which were prepared perfectly. Clint learned that Diane Bellamy was a local gal, had a business of her own, and couldn't often treat herself to supper at the steakhouse, but tonight had decided to splurge.

"Then you'll have dessert when we're done," he said, "because I'm paying."

"Oh no!" she said, looking distressed. "That wasn't my intention when I came over here—"

"I know that," he assured her, "but I appreciate the company. I'm new in town. This is my first day."

"How long do you plan to stay?" she asked. "I can show you around."

"Not long, I'm afraid," Clint said. "I only found this place because the sheriff recommended it."

"Oh, you know the sheriff?" she asked. "Are you friends?"

"No," Clint said, "we only just met, in fact."

"Are you a lawman?" she asked.

"No," he said, "my name's Clint Adams. I . . . just sort of . . . drift."

"A drifter?" she said. "I don't think so. Clint Adams." She nodded. "I know the name. I can't say I ever expected to have supper with The Gunsmith."

"I hope you're not disappointed."

"Not at all," she said. "This steak is excellent. And I think I will take you up on the offer of dessert."

"Very good," Clint said, going back to his own steak.

***

Clint chose peach pie for dessert, and had to forgive Diane for choosing rhubarb, his least favorite. They washed it down with good, strong coffee.

After Clint paid the bill they stepped outside, where dusk was falling.

"Where are you off to?" she asked.

"The sheriff said something about a Red Roan Saloon?" he answered.

"Ah," she said, "that's a very popular place—with men. Lots of drinking and gambling."

He laughed.

"I like drinking and gambling, sometimes."

"Well," she said, "if you'll agree to walk me home, I think I can show you an even better place."

"That's not an offer I can pass up, is it?" he asked. "The Red Roan can wait until later."

She smiled and said, "This way, then."

***

They strolled through the streets of Des Moines as it got dark. Clint wondered if he was wasting valuable time or, if not here, would he have just been killing time in his room?

She walked him to a neighborhood of one-story houses, one of which belonged to her. Many of them were white, but hers was painted blue, with a blue picket fence around it.

He followed her up the path to the front door, waited while she unlocked it.

"Well," she said, "I'm home."

"I thought you said you were going to show me a better place than the Red Roan," he reminded her.

"I am," she said. "It's in here." She stepped inside.

Clint looked around, didn't see anyone else on the street. This could have been a seduction, or a trap. If it was seduction, he was all for it. If it was a trap, he wanted to know who had set it, and why?

He followed her inside.

***

The house was dark. That supported seduction, but did not eliminate a trap. He saw a light toward the back of the house and headed for it.

He didn't hear anything ahead of him, and as his eyes grew accustomed to the darkness of the house, he saw nothing around him. He was prepared to draw his gun at a moment's notice.

When he reached the doorway where the light was emanating from, he saw that it was her bedroom. He hoped to find only Diane in the room.

As he entered, he pushed the door all the way open, so he could be sure no one was hiding behind it. As he did he saw her standing over by a dressing screen, wearing a robe. She had managed to undress very quickly. He wondered when she had started planning all this.

She turned then, acted surprised to see him there. Either that, or she was surprised to see him ready to pull his gun.

“You won’t need that,” she said. “I promise.”

“Sorry,” he said, “I couldn’t be sure.”

“Of what?” she said, and then, “Oh, you mean . . . you thought this might be a trap?”

“Diane, I—”

“No, no,” she said, “I understand, with your reputation, and all. I guess it is a trap—” she dropped her robe to the floor, revealing herself to be naked underneath, “though not the kind you were thinking.”

Chapter Twenty-Six

He found himself rooted to the floor, staring at her. Luckily, nobody came into the room behind him and shot him in the back.

But a trap was still not out of the question.

She had an ornate bedpost that was not conducive to hanging a holster. So he pulled a chair over to the bed and set the holster there.

"Feel safer?" she asked.

"For now."

"Then get your clothes off," she said. "I'm impatient. I've finally found a decent man."

"I appreciate the compliment."

"Don't," she said, "not until I know if you're as skilled as you are decent."

She approached him and began to unbutton his shirt. The heat from her bountiful body was intense. The brown nipples of her large breasts were swelling, and as she removed his shirt she brushed them against the skin of his chest.

They worked together to remove his boots and strip him naked, and then he gave in to the urge to touch her. Her flesh was smooth and fulfilled the promise of the heat she was generating. She was scalding.

She reached up to wrap her arms around his neck and draw him down to her mouth. They kissed, and he forgot about any kind of a trap. Her mouth was too avid for her not to be completely genuine about the kiss.

He ran his hands down her back, took one buttock in each hand and held her even closer. His penis swelled until it felt like it would burst.

"We'd better get to bed," she said, "before one of us explodes."

"No argument from me."

They gravitated toward the bed together and fell onto it while still in a heated embrace. Their legs intertwined, their hands roamed, their mouths fused. Suddenly, and with surprising strength, she rolled him onto his back and straddled him.

"Don't you want to know when I planned this?" she asked, looking down at him. Her black hair fell, framed her lovely face.

"Actually," he said, "no, but . . . you planned this? Before I got to the steakhouse?"

"No," she said, "I planned it the moment you entered the steakhouse."

"Why?"

"Because you were a stranger," she said. "Because I'd never seen you before, and you'd never seen me."

"And that was important?" he asked, running a finger around one nipple and then the other.

"I've lived in this town all my life," she said. "I've turned down most of the eligible men. I can't just sleep with anyone. And then . . . there you were."

"So the fact that I'm . . . who I am . . . had nothing to do with your decision?"

She smiled.

"Well," she said, "it may have had something to do with my final decision. I mean, once we started to dine together, and talk, it was an easier decision to make."

"And now that you've made the decision," he asked, "do you want to keep talking?"

"No," Diane said, "no, I don't want to talk anymore. I just want to go and go . . .

She reached down to take hold of his hard cock, pressed the head to her vagina, and sat on it, taking it inside. If he thought the heat from the outside of her body was intense, he had no words for the way she felt inside.

"Diane—"

"Shut up," she said, starting to move up and down on him, "no more talking . . .

Chapter Twenty-Seven

Clint had run into this kind of thing in other towns. Women who had standing in their community, who felt they could not be seen sleeping with the prominent men in town—or the ones lower on the totem pole. They needed to find someone who was there for a short time, and, would soon be gone. Very often, the Gunsmith fit that bill.

At the moment, he was fitting very well inside of Diane Bellamy, and she was riding him up and down for all she was worth. Her breasts bounced in front of his face, which he enjoyed for as long as he could before having to reach out and clutch at them. He was just unable to resist.

When he grabbed her breasts, and his thumbs touched her nipples, she grabbed his wrists, as if to hold them there. Then, suddenly, she came down on him and stayed down, started grinding while gritting her teeth and grunting.

He felt her insides quivering and trembling and grabbing at him, he felt her gush, wetting his thighs and the bed beneath them, and then instead of collapsing on top of him as other women had done, she suddenly leaped off him and said, "Move over!"

She moved him to the side, away from the wet area of the bed, and then got down between his legs and began to lick the length of his cock. First she lapped off all of her own juices, and then went on to thoroughly wet it with her saliva. When it was gleaming she opened her mouth and took it all the way in.

Clint did all he could not to yell, even though he doubted anyone would be around to hear him. He reached down to touch her head as she bobbed up and down, her mouth and teeth gliding over him, inflaming him even more. At one point he felt as if he was ready to explode, and tried to withdraw from her mouth, but she made a muffled objection and, finally, he simply erupted into her mouth . . .

***

Later, she actually made him get off the bed so she could change the sheets, and then they reclined on the fresh, dry ones, with her head on his left shoulder so that his right hand was still free.

"So?" she asked.

"So what?"

"As traps go, how was that one?"

"That was my kind of trap," he said, "definitely."

She smiled, reached her hand down so she could hold his now semi-hard penis. After a moment, he heard her dozing . . .

***

Partridge entered the room to collect the tray he had brought in with Verne's supper on it. The French writer had eaten everything.

"Was that okay?" Partridge asked.

"Zat was excellent," Verne said. "Zank you. Is zees how well you feed kidnap victims here in the West?"

"I dunno," Partridge said. "I ain't never kidnapped nobody before."

"Zo, what will we be doing next?" Verne asked.

"We're gonna be leavin' town."

"Ah, zat is excellent. Will we be going west?"

"That's gonna be up to Train," Partridge said. "He's makin' all the plans, but yeah, I think we will. Why?"

"Because, *mon ami,* zat is where I want to go," Jules Verne said. "I want to see the West."

"What's that mean?" Partridge asked.

"Pardon?"

"What you called me," Partridge said. "Money-me? What is that?"

"Ah, *mon ami,"* Verne said. "Zat is French for 'my friend.'"

"But . . . I kidnapped you," Partridge said. "Why are you callin' me your friend?"

"Are you planning to kill me?" Verne asked.

"What? No, I ain't gonna kill ya."

Verne shrugged.

"Then why can we not be friends?"

Partridge was confused. He turned and headed for the door with the tray. He opened it, and turned.

"I'll bring you some coffee."

"*Merci, mon ami*," Verne said. "Thank, you, my friend."

***

When Partridge entered the livingroom of the house they were occupying Train looked up at him.

"Did he eat?"

"Yeah, he ate."

"Good," Train said. "We've got to keep his strength up."

"Are we gonna kill 'im?" Partridge asked.

"Wha—no, we ain't gonna kill 'im. Why would you ask me that?"

"*He* asked *me* that."

"Why?"

"He called me his friend," Partridge said. "I asked him why and he asked if we were gonna kill 'im. When I said, no, he said, 'Then why can't be friends?' or somethin' like that. He called me money-me."

"What the hell is that?"

"He says it means 'my friend.'"

"So he's cooperatin'"

"Not only that," Partridge said, "he says he wants to go west."

"Then good," Train said. "If we have to be his friends to get him to go along, let's do it."

"I told 'im I'd bring him some coffee."

"Then do it. We might as well keep Frenchie happy."

Chapter Twenty-Eight

And while Train and Partridge were keeping "Frenchie" happy, Clint was doing his best to keep Diane happy.

She had only dozed for a few minutes, and when she woke, she was ready for more. So he gave it to her.

It was his turn to slide down between her legs, lick and suck until she was good and wet and writhing, and then ride up on her and drive his cock deep into her. She gasped, her eyes wide, and then wrapped her powerful legs around his waist. They remained locked that way as he continued to pump into her until he, once again, exploded . . .

***

"Do you have to go?" she asked, as he dressed. She was lying on her back with the sheet covering her, but molded to her.

"Yes," he said. "There are things I have to do."

"And I've been distracting you?"

"Definitely."

"What's so important?" she asked.

"There's a man I have to find," he said. "His safety is my responsibility."

"And you have to do this alone?"

"I hope not," he said. "I'll find that out tomorrow."

He walked to the bed, leaned down and kissed her, and then hurriedly left her bedroom, and the house, before he changed his mind.

***

When he got back to his hotel he washed up with the pitcher-and-basin, and got into his bed. He needed to get some sleep to be ready for whatever was coming. He was prepared to do whatever he had to do to find Jules Verne and secure his safety. He only hoped Jim West was right about help coming, and soon.

***

When he woke, he dressed quickly and went downstairs for breakfast. He hoped to find a message waiting for him at the front desk, but there wasn't one. He went into the dining room to have his breakfast, but ate it quickly so he could return to the lobby. He was depending on Jim West's word, and wanted to be available when the help arrived. That was when he saw the man enter the hotel.

Not Jim West.

But Jeremy Pike.

***

Pike was a secret service agent who often worked with Jim West and his partner, Artie Gordon. He had also worked with Clint several times, so the two men knew each other on sight. They did not, however, give away that fact as soon as they saw each other. Instead, Pike crossed the lobby and entered the hotel bar, which had only just opened its doors.

Clint gave Pike a few moments to pick a spot in the bar, and then entered, himself. There was one man standing at the bar, receiving a beer from the bartender. Pike was seated at a table well away from both the door and the bar, drinking a cup of coffee.

Clint went to the bar.

"'mornin', sir," the bartender said.

"Good-morning. Can I have a cup of coffee, please?"

"Comin' up."

As Clint waited for the coffee, Jeremy Pike spoke up from his table.

"Excuse me," he called out.

Both Clint and the other man at the bar turned to see who he was speaking to.

"Yes, you," Pike said, gesturing toward Clint, "I just arrived in town. I wonder if you could help me out?"

"I'll try," Clint returned, "although I only arrived yesterday."

"Well, then," Pike said, "we're in the same boat, aren't we?"

Clint accepted the coffee from the bartender with a nod of thanks, then walked over to Pike's table.

"Have a seat," Pike said, loudly.

Clint sat across from the secret service agent.

"Hello, Clint," Pike said.

"Jeremy," Clint said. "Been a while. How's Jim?"

"Off busy, as usual, but he got your message, and I happened to be spitting distance from here, so here I am. How can I help?"

"Jules Verne," Clint said. "Do you know who he is?"

"I do," Pike said. "I read the Captain Nemo book—what was it?—Twenty Thousand Leagues?"

"Well, he's in the country . . ." Clint said, and went to explain how he had met Verne, and what the French author had asked him to do.

"Well," Pike said, "you didn't get very far west before trouble hit, did you?"

"No, we didn't."

"Any idea who snatched him?"

"Two men on the train named Partridge and Train seem likely," Clint said. "The conductor thought they were up to something."

"Like what?"

"He thought they were intending to rob the train, but if they were, they changed their minds when they realized who Verne was."

"So they decided on kidnapping rather than train robbery?" Pike said. "Either way they're in trouble."

"They're in trouble," Clint said, "if and when we catch them."

"Did you see the men?" Pike asked. "Can you identify them?"

"I saw them, but I got their names from the conductor, who got them from their tickets," Clint explained. "I don't know which is which."

"Well, I guess I can see why I'm here," Pike said. "As a representative of the government. If anything happens to Verne, it'll be an international incident."

"And all my fault," Clint said.

Rather than try to ease Clint's guilt Pike said, "Well, there is that," and sipped his coffee.

Chapter Twenty-Nine

"Well," Pike said, "I have to check in with Washington and let them know I'm here. For now they're only going to want me to take an observer's stance, but Jim West wanted me to actually come and help. So you just have to let me know what you want me to do."

"Get yourself situated," Clint said, "and check in with D.C., and then we'll go from there."

"What's your best guess about what they're going to do?" Pike asked, as they prepared to leave.

"If it was me," Clint said, "I'd get out of Des Moines, so I'm going to check today with some of the liveries. They're going to need three horses, or a wagon."

"Can Verne ride?"

"He said yes, but I haven't had a chance to find out," Clint said. "Hopefully, he can't, and that'll hold them up."

They stood and walked to the lobby together.

"Does it matter to you if I get a room here at the same hotel as you?" Pike asked.

"Doesn't matter at all," Clint said. "If I'm right, we won't be here much longer, anyway."

***

"You were supposed to keep him busy all night and all day," Dan Train said.

"I tried," Diane Bellamy said. "I had him in my bed most of the night."

Train looked around. He didn't know Diane Bellamy very well, but he did know that she was the kind of girl who hired out for different kinds of jobs. When he and Partridge arrived in Des Moines, he looked her up invoking the name of a mutual friend.

Of course, "Diane Bellamy" was not her real name. Train had been told that this woman was as good at the con game as they got, and all he needed was for her to con Clint Adams for a day. Apparently, she couldn't even do that.

"So you still expect me to pay you?" Train asked.

As far as she was concerned, he didn't have to pay her, at all, for what she had done last night. The time she had spent in bed with Clint Adams had been unmatched by any sex she'd had in the past. In fact, she had become so involved with what they had been doing that she couldn't even call it a con. There was no way the Gunsmith could have questioned her commitment, because once they got started, she forgot all about looking at him as a "job."

But she couldn't let this man know that she had lost her professionalism when it came to Clint Adams.

"You wanted me to occupy him, and I did," she said. "Granted, not all day, so I tell you what. I'll settle for half of what we agreed on."

Train looked around the small café they were using as a meeting place, and then pushed an envelope across the table at her.

"You already figured that," she said.

"Half is about what you earned," he agreed.

"Well," she said, taking the envelope off the table, "if he's any kind of normal man, he ain't walkin' all that well today. His legs have gotta be weak."

Train pushed his chair back.

"Have another cup of coffee," he said. "I don't want us to be seen together."

"Are you leavin' town today?" she asked.

"Never mind," he said, standing.

She watched him leave, then sat back, stuffed the envelope into her drawstring purse, and waved at the waiter for another coffee. She didn't know about Clint Adams' legs, but hers were still pretty weak. She hoped to never run into that kind of man again. She didn't need to ever be out of control like that. Not when her business was the con.

Chapter Thirty

They split in the lobby, Pike to the desk to get a room, and Clint to the street to start checking livery stables.

As Clint started down the street, he saw Sheriff Lariman walking toward him. The man spotted him and waved.

"I was just comin' to your hotel to check in with you," Lariman said.

"I appreciate that," Clint said, "but I've got nothing to report."

"Where are you off to, then?"

"I was going to start checking some of the liveries, see if anybody bought any horses this morning, or a wagon."

"You thinkin' they'll leave town?"

"That's what I'd do," Clint said, "get Verne out of Des Moines and hidden someplace."

"Well, we've got about half a dozen liveries," the sheriff said. "If you wanna split 'em, we can take three each."

"I appreciate the offer, but I think I'm going to check them all myself."

"Suit yourself, then," the sheriff said, slightly miffed. He was probably thinking that Clint didn't trust him, completely—and he was right.

With Pike in town to help him, Clint decided he couldn't put his confidence in anyone else.

"Maybe you can help me with something else," Clint said.

"What's that?"

"Do you know a woman named Diane Bellamy?"

"The name's not familiar," Lariman said. "Is she local?"

"She's supposed to be."

"Can't help ya," Lariman said, "and if you don't need my help with the stables, I guess I'll get to my rounds."

"Sheriff, I didn't mean any offense," Clint said. "I just think this is my responsibility."

Slightly mollified, Lariman said, "I guess I can understand that. I wish you luck."

They went their separate ways, and Clint decided on one more stop before checking the liveries.

***

Second thoughts were niggling at the back of Clint's brain. They involved Diane Bellamy, who had come to him from out of nowhere. Sure, he had dallied with women at first meeting before, but this felt different, for some reason. Maybe *too* planned . . .

He left the sheriff and walked to the house Diane had taken him to. It was easy to find, as it stood out like a blue thumb on a white hand.

He walked up to the front door and knocked. When there was no answer, he looked around to make sure no one was watching him, and then put his shoulder to the door, forcing it open. It was dim inside, but he could see. And what he could see he couldn't have seen last night. There was a blanket of dust on everything around him. He walked through the house to the bedroom she had taken him to. It was the only room where the dust had been disturbed.

No one lived in this house.

Just to be sure, he went through the rest of the house, including the kitchen. There was no sign that anyone had cooked there for months.

It *had* been a trap. But not the deadly kind. She was probably supposed to keep him busy for as long as she could, maybe as far into the day if possible. Only he had left in the morning, spoiling the plan.

He went back out the front door and left the area. He was now sure the kidnappers were planning to leave Des Moines that morning, and were hoping he would be otherwise occupied. He had to take advantage of the fact that the plan hadn't worked.

He headed back to his hotel.

***

He knocked on Jeremy Pike's door and waited. When it opened, he slipped in, and Pike closed the door.

"What's up?"

"My cock almost got us in trouble."

"What?"

He explained about Diane Bellamy, and the night he spent at that house.

"And the house is empty this morning?" Pike asked.

"Completely."

"Okay," Pike said, "no use crying over spilled milk, or beating yourself up. Let's find out where they're getting their transportation, horses or a wagon."

"Right."

"How many liveries are there?"

"The sheriff told me there are six."

"All right," Pike said, "let's split them up."

Pike grabbed his jacket, strapped on his gun, and they left the room.

In the lobby Clint went to the desk clerk, who gave him the location of all six livery stables within the town limits of Des Moines.

"There'll be some outside," he added.

"This will have to do for now," Clint said. "Thanks."

He walked toward Pike and tore the piece of paper the clerk had written the locations on in half.

"Yours," he said, handing half to Pike.

"Right. Meet back here in an hour?"

"Or as close to that as we can get," Clint said. "I don't know how far apart these stables are."

"Gotcha."

Chapter Thirty-One

"Can you ride?" Train asked Jules Verne, as they approached the livery stable.

"I have ridden."

"That doesn't answer my question," Train said. "I don't want to use a buggy. You're gonna have to ride, western style, not some French style."

"There is no French style," Verne said. "I will ride."

Train looked at Partridge.

"Get us three horses," he told him.

"Right. How much do I—"

"Don't dicker," Train said. "After we ransom this fella, we'll have plenty of money."

Partridge nodded and went around the corner to the livery stable.

"May I ask a question?" Verne asked.

"Sure, go ahead," Train said.

"How much will you be asking for my return?"

"None of your business," Train said.

"And who will you be asking to pay," Verne asked, "my government, or yours?"

"Why are you askin' so many questions?" Train asked.

"I am just trying to be helpful."

"We kidnapped you," Train said. "Why do you wanna help us?"

"You are going to show me zee West," Verne said. "I am grateful."

"Jesus," Train said, "you're crazy. Just shut up for a while."

"Very well, *mon ami*," Verne said. "I will shut up."

"And don't call me that 'money-me" crap!"

***

Partridge came back around the corner leading three horses, fully outfitted. Train noticed a spot of blood on his shirt.

"Did he dicker?" Train asked.

"He tried. We're gonna need some supplies," he said, handing Train the reins.

"We can't," Train said. "Not here. Adams is gonna be looking for us to outfit."

"So he'll find out about these horses," Partridge said.

"We'll be gone by the time he does," Train said. "But if we stop to get supplies, we'll lose our head start."

Train turned to Jules Verne and handed him the reins of one of the horses.

"Mount up!"

***

Clint walked into the lobby of the hotel two hours later. Pike wasn't there. He had checked three liveries, and no one had brought three horses. Now he had to see what Pike had discovered.

He sat on a lobby divan to wait, but it didn't take long. Pike came walking in ten minutes later and joined him.

"Anything?" Clint asked.

"No," Pike said. "You?"

"Nothing."

"So now what?"

"The desk clerk said there were some liveries outside of town."

"I guess we'll have to check those next."

They stood up, but before they could move, the desk clerk came running over to them. He was a small man in his forties, and he was wringing his hands, looking alarmed.

"I'm so sorry!" he said.

"About what?"

"I forgot," he said. "I forgot one. It's a private livery, and it's on Randolph Street."

"Is that the only one you forgot?" Clint asked.

"That's it." He handed Clint a slip of paper. "Here's the address."

Clint and Pike left the lobby, but the secret service agent stopped outside.

"What is it?" Clint asked.

"You trust him?"

"The clerk?" Clint asked. "I don't trust anybody except you, Jeremy, but he's got no reason to lie that I can see."

"Okay," Pike said, "it's your call."

They waved down a passing cab.

***

They left the cab in front of the livery stable on Randolph Street.

"Front door's locked," Pike said, trying it.

He pounded on it, but got no answer.

"Let's try the back."

They went around back together, found a door, tried it and entered. It was dark inside. There were several horses in stalls, and a few empty ones. The corral in back was empty.

"Anybody here?" Clint called.

No answer. And then a moan.

"Over there," Pike said, moving toward an empty stall.

Clint followed, found Pike leaning over a fallen man.

"He's been stabbed," Pike said.

"Bad?"

Pike looked at Clint and shook his head. There was nothing to be done. The old hostler would be dead soon.

"Ask him," Clint said.

"My friend," Pike said, "what happened? Who did this to you?"

"A man came . . . he wanted three horses . . . but wouldn't pay my price."

"And did he take them?" Pike asked.

The man nodded.

"Was an older man with them?" Clint asked. "Spoke with an accent?"

"One man," the hostler said, painfully, "there was one man . . . he-he stabbed . . ." He trailed off.

"Did they say which way they were going?" Clint asked.

Pike looked up at Clint and said, "He's dead." The secret service agent stood up. "This must've happened in the past hour or so."

"We'll have to notify the sheriff," Clint said, "then get you a horse—they're going to have a few hours head start."

"And we don't know what direction they took."

"West," Clint said.

"Are you sure?"

"No," Clint said, "but it's likely. We all came from the east, why go back that way? Besides, these two would-be bank robbers and kidnappers probably know the west better."

"I don't think we want the sheriff knowing why I'm here," Pike commented.

"You're right," Clint said. "The government never wants anyone knowing they're here. I'll go and find him, and you can go to another livery, get yourself a horse, and meet me in front of the hotel."

"Gotcha," Pike said. "An hour?"

"I hate giving them that much more of a head start," Clint said, "but yeah, an hour. It'll probably take me that long to get away from the sheriff."

"We could leave this body here for somebody else to find," Pike suggested.

Clint grimaced.

"The desk clerk knows I came here," Clint said, "and somebody else might have seen us. No, I better notify the sheriff, myself. While we're tracking the kidnappers, we don't need anybody tracking us."

"Okay, then," Pike said, "in front of the hotel in an hour."

Clint nodded.

"See you there."

Chapter Thirty-Two

Clint found the sheriff making his rounds and convinced him to accompany him to the livery.

"What's goin' on, Adams?" Lariman asked, just outside the building.

"Got bad news for you inside," Clint said, as they entered through the back door.

"Jesus," Lariman said, when he saw the man lying in the stall. "That's Jack Lester. This is his place." He looked at Clint. "Did you do this?"

"He was stabbed," Clint said. "That's not my style. No, the kidnappers were here, only now they're killers."

"You got proof?"

"Before he died this man told me he was stabbed by a man who came in to buy three horses."

"So you want me to get up a posse to chase . . . who? We don't even know which way they're headed."

"You can do what you like," Clint said. "I felt I had to tell you about this killing. Now I'm going to head west and try tracking them. I figure they're probably headed for Council Bluffs."

"With your French writer?"

"That's right."

"You figure puttin' him on a horse will slow them down?"

"I hope so," Clint said. "I really don't know what kind of rider he is."

Lariman looked down at the dead hostler.

"I'm not comfortable about lettin' you leave town," the lawman said. "And the chief-of-police won't like it, either."

"You're going to tell him?"

"I gotta," Lariman said. "I was told when they opened their new police department that I could keep my job as long as I worked with them."

"Okay," Clint said, "all I ask is that you let me get started before you tell the chief. When I catch up to them, I'll get my writer back, and I'll make sure you get your killers."

"All you got are names," Lariman reminded him.

"I'm sure Verne will have something to say about the killing," Clint said. "He'll be your witness."

"If he comes out of this alive."

"He better," Clint said, "or we're going to have a couple of very unhappy governments."

"All right," Sheriff Lariman said, after some thought, "how long do you need?"

Chapter Thirty-Three

Clint collected Eclipse from the livery where he had boarded him and rode over to the hotel. He found Pike waiting in front, with a large grey roan he had rented or bought.

"Finished with the sheriff?" Pike asked.

"For now," Clint said. "It took some talking, but I got him to agree to let me leave town before he has to tell the chief-of-police what's going on."

"I saw that building," Pike said, "wondered if we were going to have to deal with that new department."

"We will," Clint said, "after we catch our kidnappers-turned-killers."

"Then let's get started," Pike said. "I hope you've got some ideas."

"A few," Clint said. "I'm figuring they'll head for Council Bluffs, find someplace to settle in before they decide to make their demands."

"And make their demands to who?" Pike asked.

"Probably the only person they'll be able to think of," Clint said, "will be me."

"And you won't be here."

"That'll stump them for a while," Clint said, "maybe long enough for us to find them."

As Clint started to mount up Pike put his hand out to stop him.

"What about just waiting here to hear from them?" he asked.

"I considered that," Clint said. "That's going to be what they want. If I'm not here, they'll have to think again."

"They could send a demand directly to Washington D.C.," Pike offered.

"They could," Clint said, "but that's still going to take them a while to figure out. I still think our best bet is to head west."

"Okay, it's your call," Pike said. "I'm just here to back you."

"And represent the government," Clint said. "We don't want the French to think we didn't look after their man."

"Then let's do the best we can to get him back in one piece," Pike said.

They mounted up and rode out of town, with only their canteens and some beef jerky to sustain them.

***

"Where are we goin'?" Partridge asked Dan Train.

"We're headin' for Council Bluffs," Train said. "I don't know if we'll get there. We might find a good place between here and there, that we can operate from, send our demands."

"To Adams? In Des Moines?"

"I'd send them to Washington, D.C. if I knew who to address them to," Train said. "Adams is gonna have to do."

They both looked over at Verne, who had dismounted and was rubbing his butt with both hands. He was still wearing a suit, but it was disheveled and dirty.

"Adams will give us whatever we want to get this man back," Train said.

"I hope you're right," Partridge said. "What about some supplies?"

"Next town we come to that has a general store or a trading post, we'll get some," Train said. "But not too much. I don't want anythin' slowin' us down."

Partridge looked over at Verne, again.

"Don't look so worried," Train said. "This is gonna go all our way."

"He's so damn calm," Partridge said.

"Good. That's better than havin' him panic and try to get away."

"I guess so."

Train put his hand on Partridge's shoulder

"You keep guessin' so and let me make the decisions," he said.

"I can make decisions, Dan," Partridge said.

"Yeah, I know," Train said, "your last decision was to kill that hostler. We'll be lucky if there's not a posse after us."

"A posse wouldn't know who to chase," Partridge reminded him.

"You sure he was dead when you left him?"

"He was dead," Partridge said. "I gutted him good."

Train patted Partridge's shoulder, then removed his hand.

"Let's hope you're right," he said. "Come on, let's get Frenchie back on his horse."

***

"There were some fresh tracks leaving that livery," Clint told Pike, as they rode out. "Three horses. If it's the right three, I might be able to track them."

"How do you tell them from other tracks?" Pike asked. "And remember, I'm a city boy."

"Horse's hooves often have unique patterns," Clint said. "It only takes one. One of these horses must've been shoed in a hurry, because it looks like the left rear is on slightly crooked."

“You noticed that?”

“I was looking closely.”

Pike looked at the road beneath them, which led out of Des Moines. All he could see was what looked like hundreds of different tracks, many of which had been run over by wagon wheels.

“Not now,” Clint said, reading the man’s mind. “But once we’re away from town, the tracks should thin out. I might be able to pick out the one we want.”

“Well,” Pike said, “I know better by now than to doubt you.”

“Look,” Clint said, “if we can’t find a thing, we’ll head back and wait for the ransom demand. Those are our two options.”

“Like I said,” Pike replied, “your call.”

Chapter Thirty-Four

Miles outside of Des Moines the trails began to thin out.

Pike waited while Clint dismounted, squatted down and examined the ground.

"Anything?" he asked, after a few moments.

Clint stood up, but continued to stare down.

"I'm not seeing what I want," he said. "Not yet, anyway."

"It's too soon to give up and go back," Pike said.

"Agreed."

Clint walked back to Eclipse and mounted up.

"Let's keep heading west."

***

"I should have let you pick out my horse," Pike said, later, as they were resting.

"The roan is fine," Clint said. "Resting him is no problem."

"I'm holding you and Eclipse back," Pike said.

"I can't ride any faster and still track," Clint said, "so no, you're not."

Pike patted the roan's neck as he fed on some grass. Eclipse kept his head up, looking ahead.

"It's over a hundred miles to Council Bluffs," Clint observed. "They might stop somewhere in-between."

"What would be likely?"

"They might pick a town with a hotel and a saloon," Clint said. "Or, a town with neither of those."

"But they'll need a telegraph," Pike said, "in order to make their demands."

"Right," Clint said. "So they'll have to be near a town with a telegraph."

"Any idea how many there are between here and Council Bluffs?"

"No," Clint said. "I've been this way before, but I can't answer that. We'll just have to wait and see as we go along."

"Meanwhile," Pike said, "you can keep looking for that crooked shoe."

"Agreed."

***

"Stay here," Train told Partridge, "with the horses, and with him." He jerked his head at Jules Verne, who was looking up and down the street of the small town.

"Yeah, okay."

Train nodded, went inside the small mercantile.

"Is zees place typical of the West?" Verne asked Sam Partridge.

"Typical?" Partridge repeated. "Yeah, I guess, pretty much like most small towns."

"How many people live here?" the writer asked.

"Probably no more than twenty."

"How do zey survive?"

"Probably through this place," Partridge said, indicating the mercantile.

"Are we robbing it?"

"Are we—no, we ain't robbin' them. We're buyin' some supplies."

"You were going to buy horses, and yet you killed zee man who owned zem."

"That was different," Partridge said.

"How?"

"Stop askin' so many damn questions!" the kidnapper snapped.

"As you wish, *mon ami*," Verne said, and continued looking up and down the small street.

***

"Are you worried about Verne?" Pike asked.

"I wasn't," Clint said, as they rode along. "He was kidnapped, they needed him alive to collect a ransom."

"But now they've killed a man," Pike added.

"That's right," Clint said. "They're no longer just kidnappers, they're killers. And that's cause for concern. We don't want to give them any reason to kill him."

"Right."

"Hold up here," Clint said.

They reined in and Clint dismounted. Once again, he crouched down to examine the ground. This time when he stood up he looked satisfied.

"This is it," he said. "I found the tracks."

"Are you sure?" Pike asked.

"Positive." Clint mounted up. "We're going to follow these tracks for as far and as long as they take us."

Pike looked over at him.

"At least now we've got a target," he said. "It'll be dark, soon."

"We'll ride as long as we've got light, then make a cold camp. We don't want them doubling back and finding us."

"Agreed."

"Let's move!"

Chapter Thirty-Five

Partridge took care of the horses while Train built a fire. They tied Verne's hands and sat him down on the ground.

"If you untie me, I can help," he said.

"Never mind," Train said. "We're fine."

He got the fire going, and then a pot of coffee. Partridge came walking over.

"Ain't you afraid somebody'll smell the coffee?" he asked. "See the fire?"

"They ain't gonna ride after dark," Train said. "And by the time they find this camp. we'll be long gone."

Partridge looked worried, but didn't say anything. He had left all the decisions up to Train—except for killing the hostler—but now he wasn't so sure he had made the right decision. On the other hand, they were too far gone to turn back.

"Sam!"

Partridge realized Train was calling him.

"Yeah?"

"Get a couple of cans of beans," Train said. "We're all hungry—ain't we, Frenchie?"

"Oh, *oui*," Verne said, "I am very hungry."

"We?" Train said, frowning.

"Yes," Verne said. "I said 'yes.'"

"Ah," Train said, as Partridge got to the fire with two cans of beans and a pan.

Verne watched as Partridge emptied the cans into the pan and put it on the fire.

"Is this a Western meal?" Verne asked. "The kind of food you would eat on a trail drive?"

"No," Sam Partridge said, "on a cattle drive there's a chuck wagon and a cook. This is just what we eat when we're camped."

"Never mind the explanations," Train said. "He'll eat what we give him."

When the beans were ready they untied Verne's hands, handed him a cup of coffee and a plate of beans.

"Eat up," Train said. "We still got a long way to go."

Verne ate enthusiastically, and asked for more.

"There you go," Partridge said, handing him another plate, "now you're eatin' like an American cowboy."

Verne smiled and dug in. He never would have expected that he would enjoy being kidnapped. He washed down a mouthful of beans with coffee, and then continued eating.

***

In their cold camp Clint and Pike supped on jerky and water from their canteens.

"They're probably camped up ahead," Pike said. "If we kept riding—"

"If we kept riding, your roan would've stepped in a chuckhole," Clint said.

"Shouldn't we be smelling their camp?" Pike asked. "Or would they be running a cold camp, as well?"

"They're upwind of us," Clint said. "If we were making coffee, they'd smell it. But they could be making coffee and bacon, and we wouldn't smell a thing."

"You could have ridden on ahead," Pike said. "Your horse wouldn't step in a chuckhole."

"Less likely," Clint said, "but there's no guarantee. I wouldn't want to risk him. Don't worry. If they're up ahead of us, we'll catch them."

"If we find a telegraph key we could check in with Des Moines and see if they tried to contact you with a demand."

"We could do that," Clint said, "but if the chief-of-police is looking for us, that'll tell him where to look."

"You don't think the sheriff 'll speak up for you?" Pike asked.

"He might, but there's no guarantee the chief will listen. I met the man. He's by the book."

"So we just keep looking," Pike said.

"We keep following that trail, as long as I can see it," Clint said.

Pike nodded. They finished their cold meal and then set watches.

"I'll take the first," Clint said, "you take the second. Just in case they double back."

"Right."

As Pike rolled himself up in his bedroll, Clint sat at the fire, wishing he had a cup of coffee.

***

Clint spent his watch thinking about Jules Verne. How could he have been so stupid as to agree to take him west? He should have insisted that the author go home, back to France where he'd be safe to write more books. But then again, it was in France that Verne had been shot by his own nephew, so how much safer would he have been there?

The only way to make sure he was safe was to find him, before the kidnappers decided he wasn't worth keeping alive.

Chapter Thirty-Six

They came to the town of Elk Horn after they had gone more than halfway to Council Bluffs.

"See that?" Train said, pointing.

"Telegraph lines," Partridge said. "Are we gonna send a telegram to Clint Adams in Des Moines?"

"That's what we're gonna do. Come on."

They rode into Elk Horn with Jules Verne between them.

"Will we be getting a hotel room? the writer asked. "With a bathtub?"

"No hotel room," Train said, "and no bath. We're just gonna send a telegram."

"How much are we askin' for?" Partridge asked.

"A hundred thousand dollars."

"Really?" Partridge asked, excited. "Do you think we can get that much?"

"Zee French government would pay more," Verne said.

Both kidnappers looked at him.

"Oh yeah?" Train asked. "How much would they pay?"

Verne shrugged and said, "I zink twice as much."

"Two hundred thousand dollars!" Partridge said, looking at Train.

"Yeah," Train said, "if we could get to the French government."

"Your government can get to my government," Verne said. "You must get Clint Adams to do it zat way."

Train rubbed his jaw and said, "He may have a point. We tell Adams to go to the United States government, and have them contact the French government with our demand."

"That's a lot of money, Dan," Partridge said. "How long would it take?"

"The first thing we gotta do is send the telegram," Train said. "Then we'll go from there."

"We're gonna have to find someplace to lay low with Frenchie, here," Partridge said.

"Right. After I send the telegram. You two just wait right here."

Partridge nodded, and Train went into the telegraph office.

"Can we get somezing to eat while we are here?" Verne asked.

"A few days on the trail and you're already tired of beans?" Partridge asked.

"I just thought—"

Like Train said, "Partridge cut him off, "we'll send the telegram, and then move on."

"So . . . nuzing?" Verne asked. "Not even a bite?"

"Nothin'," Partridge said.

***

After about twenty minutes Train came out of the telegraph office.

"What took you so long?" Partridge asked.

"I had to word it just right," Train said.

"Did you say two hundred thousand?"

"I did," Train said, "and I told Adams he should arrange to get it from Frenchie's people."

"Then we're done here?" Partridge said. "We're startin' to attract attention."

Train looked across the street, saw several people staring over at them.

"Yeah, we been standin' out here too long," he said. "Let's get outta here." He looked at Verne. "Mount up!"

Jules Verne heaved a sigh and climbed up into the saddle, which was becoming more uncomfortable as they went along, not less.

***

Clint frowned down at the ground.

"What's wrong?" Pike asked.

"They're not doing anything to hide their trail," Clint said.

"Maybe they're dumb enough to think nobody's following them," Pike suggested.

"That could be," Clint agreed.

"How fresh are these tracks?"

"Judging by the dead campfire we found a while ago, and these tracks," Clint replied, "I figure they're about half-a-day in front of us."

"If, indeed, these tracks are being left by them."

"Right," Clint said, "but we don't seem to have any other options."

"What about contacting the sheriff in Des Moines?" Pike asked. "Have you given that any more thought?"

"I'd send a telegram to the desk clerk in the hotel, if I knew his name," Clint said. "If the kidnappers sent me a telegram there, it would be at the desk."

"You still think the sheriff might turn you in to the chief?"

"I don't know," Clint said, "but I may have to contact him just to get some idea of what's happening."

"What about me contacting D.C.?" Pike asked.

"To see if the kidnappers contacted them?" Clint asked. "I don't think they'd know who to get in touch with."

"So you're elected," Pike said.

"They saw him with me," Clint said, "and they took him away from me. It makes sense they'd want to contact me."

"Only they can't because we're out here."

"So they're going to have to try to figure out what to do next," Clint said, "and while they're doing that, we're going to catch up to them."

They mounted up and started riding, again.

"What if they can't figure out their next move, and decide to kill him?"

"They won't."

"Why not? They killed the hostler."

"I have a theory about that," Clint said. "I don't think it was planned."

"They stabbed him by accident?" Pike asked.

"Not by accident," Clint said, "but I don't think it was planned."

"Why not?"

"It doesn't make sense," Clint said. "All they had to do was buy three horses."

"So why was he killed?"

Clint looked at Pike.

"We can ask them when we catch up."

Chapter Thirty-Seven

"I just thought of somethin'," Partridge said.

"We were gonna let me do the thinkin', Sam," Train reminded him.

Partridge looked over at Verne, who had dismounted and was rubbing his butt.

"I just got a question," he said.

"Okay," Train said, "ask."

"If Adams gets your telegram with our demands," Partridge said, "how's he gonna get in touch with us?"

"My telegram said he'd hear from me again, and he should have the money ready."

"But how'll we know he has the money?" Partridge asked. "And how will he get it to us?"

"No more questions, Sam," Train said. "Just relax. I've got this."

"Yeah, okay."

"Get Frenchie back on his horse."

"Sure."

Partridge walked over to where Verne was standing. Train turned his back, because he was finding both men annoying. And he was also annoyed that he hadn't yet figured how to find out if Clint Adams got the money, or not. They were going to have to find a place they could send a telegram from, and then receive one, and then get away before Adams sent the law. Or worse, came himself for them.

It was starting to look like it might have been easier to rob the train.

***

"Telegraph poles," Pike said.

"I see them," Clint said. "If we're on the right track, they probably stopped here to send a telegram."

"It's getting dark," Pike said. "We can check with the telegraph operator, spend the night and get an early start in the morning."

"Good idea," Clint said.

"Elk Horn doesn't look very big," Pike said. "I wonder why they even have a telegraph?"

"It doesn't really matter," Clint said.

"You're right," Pike said. "I'm just curious."

"Then we can ask that, too," Clint said.

They rode into Elk Horn.

***

As he dismounted in front of the telegraph office Pike asked, "What about the law?"

"Let's stay away from that, for a start," Clint suggested.

They both mounted the boardwalk and went inside.

"What can I do for you gents?" the tall, gangly clerk asked. "I'm about to close."

"We need to know if anyone sent a telegram to Des Moines in the past day or two," Clint said.

"Or to Washington, D.C.," Pike added. Clint looked at him. "Just in case."

"Right," Clint said, "or Washington, D.C."

"I can't tell ya that," the clerk said. "We don't talk 'bout our customer's telegrams."

"You'll talk about this one," Pike said, showing the man his identification.

"The United States Government?" the clerk asked, his eyes widening.

"That's right," Pike said.

"What the heck are you doin' in Elk Horn?"

"Looking for kidnappers," Pike said. "What's a telegraph line doing in Elk Horn?"

"There are a lot of ranchers in the area who wanted a telegraph key close by," the clerk said. "They all put up the money."

"That answers that question," Clint said, "now answer our first one."

"Des Moines, you said?" the clerk asked.

"Or Washington, D.C.," Pike added.

The clerk turned and began leafing through a sheaf of flimsy copies, finally pulling one out.

"Here's one for Des Moines," he said, handing it over. "It's to Clint Adams, at a hotel in Des Moines. Uh, is that the Gunsmith?"

"It is," Pike said, as he and Clint read the telegram.

"And is one of you the Gunsmith?"

"Yes," Pike said, but didn't bother to point out which one. After all, he'd just shown the clerk his own i.d.

Clint and Pike moved away from the front desk and the clerk, but remained inside.

"Two hundred thousand," Pike said.

"These fellas are crazy," Clint said.

"Maybe not," Pike said. "It's a good suggestion, getting the money from the French government."

"It's not signed." Clint lowered the telegram and looked at Pike.

"Do they even know that we have their names?"

"I guess it doesn't matter. Would you know who to contact in D.C. to get this started?" Clint asked. "I mean, just in case."

"We'd have to let it be known that Jules Verne's been kidnapped," Pike said.

"Would it get you in trouble for not saying something before this?"

"Not necessarily," Pike said. "I can just claim I was nearby when it happened, and I'm looking into it."

Clint thought a moment, then said, "Okay, send it."

"Are we going to wait for a reply?"

"Is it likely we'll get one immediately?"

"Considering the international implications?" Pike said. "I think so."

"Let's do it, then get a couple of hotel rooms."

Pike stepped forward, gave the clerk back the telegram, then got himself a pencil and blank piece of paper to write his own.

"I'll keep it as brief as possible," Pike said. "Let them know what's happening, and ask for instructions."

"Fine," Clint said. "After this we can get a drink."

Pike finished writing and handed the telegram to the clerk.

"Where's the nearest saloon?" Clint asked.

"The Panhandle, down the street," the clerk said.

"And hotel?"

"Between here and there," the clerk said. "It's called The Iowa House."

"We'll likely be in the saloon when a reply comes in," Clint said.

"What if there ain't a reply?"

"There will be," Pike said.

The clerk shrugged, and Clint and Pike left the office, confident that the clerk might close the office, but he'd also wait for their reply.

Chapter Thirty-Eight

Over a beer at the Panhandle Saloon Clint said, "I think maybe I've played this all wrong."

"Do you think you should've just waited in Des Moines for the ransom demand?"

"No," Clint said, "I'm going further back than that. I never should have agreed to take Verne west."

"If you hadn't," Pike asked, "would he have done it, anyway?"

"Probably."

"And with somebody less reliable than you."

Clint drank his beer, still not convinced. He looked around the small saloon, which wasn't very busy, despite the late hour. They had gotten two rooms at the Iowa House before adjourning to the saloon to await their reply from D.C.

"Any stranger been through here of late?" Pike asked the bartender.

"Just you two," the bored man said.

"They must have only stopped to send that telegram," Pike said.

"So they're getting a little further ahead of us," Clint said.

"They're going to have to give us a location if they want their money," Pike pointed out.

"These are not smart fellas, considering they were planning to rob a train at a time when the last major train job was eighteen-seventy-seven on the Union Pacific in Nebraska. I don't think they even scouted it, since they didn't know I was on the train."

"That didn't stop them from pulling a kidnapping," Pike said.

"True, but I still don't think they're smart enough to pull this off."

"We'll just have to wait and see how they intend to collect their money," Pike said. "Hopefully, they'll pick out a place for the exchange that we can work with."

They ordered a second beer each when the batwings opened, and the telegraph clerk came in. He spotted them and rushed over.

"Here's that answer you was lookin' for," he said, handing the telegram to Pike. "I guess they work late in Washington, too."

"Thanks." Pike gave the clerk a coin.

"Thank you, sir."

As the clerk left Pike read the telegram.

"From my boss, the head of the secret service."

"Do I know him?"

"I doubt it," Pike said. "He was appointed last month. Raymond J. Giles, a politician from top to bottom."

"What's he got to say?"

"He wants me to keep on it, and he'll go through channels to the French government." Pike looked at Clint. "Tells me to stay in touch."

"What great advice," Clint said.

They accepted their beers from the bartender and paid.

"Let's finish these and get to the hotel," Clint said. "I want to get an early start in the morning."

"Suits me," Pike said. "I could use a real bed."

They drank them down and left the saloon to walk to the hotel. As they approached the front of the building, there was a sudden volley of shots from across the street.

Neither man had to tell the other what to do. They both hit the ground and rolled, looking for cover. Clint came to a stop behind a horse trough, and Pike a nearby buckboard.

"What the hell—" Pike snapped.

"Looks like they're in the shadows right across the street," Clint said. "I'm going to draw their fire so we can see their muzzle flashes, and then we'll take it to them."

"I'm ready," Pike said.

Clint rose up from behind the trough, and the firing began.

Chapter Thirty-Nine

Clint and Pike concentrated their return fire on the muzzle flashes from across the street. There had to be at least four shooters. This couldn't have anything to do with the kidnapping of Jules Verne. Why would the kidnappers set this kind of trap for them? Kill them and they might not get paid.

This was something else.

The firing stopped. They were probably reloading, so Clint and Pike did the same.

"Ready?" Clint asked.

"I'm ready," Pike said. "What am I ready for?"

"Let's charge them," Clint said.

"Really?"

"Yes," Clint said. They were close enough to hear each other, but far enough across the street that the shooters couldn't hear them. "We could just sit here and wait for them to get tired of shooting at us, but I want to find out why they're doing this."

"You don't think it's the kidnappers?"

"No," Clint said.

"Why do you want to charge them?"

"Because they're firing wildly, now," Clint said. "We charge them, and they'll panic."

"Okay, then," Pike said. "This is your bailiwick. You say go."

"Right." Clint got into a crouch. "Ready? Go!"

They both broke from cover and ran toward the site of the muzzle flashes. As Clint predicted, the shooters began firing wildly, not even coming close to hitting them. As Clint and Pike got closer the figures in the shadows became distinctive. When the two fired, it wasn't wildly, but accurately.

"I want one of them alive!" Clint shouted.

As they reached the other side of the street two men broke from their cover and began to run. Two others were lying prone on the boardwalk. Pike shot one of the fleeing men, but Clint chased the other one and tackled him. They both fell from the boardwalk into the street.

"Hold it!" Clint snapped, as the man started to get up to run. He stopped and raised his hands.

There was the sound of running toward them, and then a voice called out, "What the hell is going on?"

It looked like Clint and Pike were not going to be able to avoid the law in Elk Horn, after all.

***

The sheriff came out of the cell block, looked at Clint and Pike seated in front of his desk.

"He says he and his friends were gonna rob you. He said they heard you have two hundred thousand dollars." The lawman, in his fifties, frowned at them. "Do you have two hundred thousand dollars?"

"Not on us," Clint said.

Pike took out his identification and showed it to the sheriff, whose name was Murphy.

"Secret Service?"

"We're working on a kidnapping," Pike said. "The ransom demand is two hundred thousand dollars and was sent from your telegraph office."

"Are the kidnappers still in town?" Murphy asked.

"No," Clint said, "they sent the telegram, and left."

"Who did they kidnap?"

"Jules Verne," Clint said.

"And who's that?"

"He's a writer," Pike said, "from France. This could turn into an international incident."

"An international . . .?"

". . . incident," Pike said. "His country could get very upset with our country."

"So these fellas heard about the two hundred thousand dollars, and thought you had it."

"Yes," Pike said.

"Jesus," Murphy said. "Three men died for bein' stupid."

"Lots of men die for that very reason," Clint said.

Chapter Forty

Sheriff Murphy let them go.

"And I'd like you to leave town tomorrow."

"That was our plan," Clint said.

"You don't need us to prosecute the prisoner?"

"No," Murphy said. "I'll take care of it."

So Clint and Pike left the sheriff's office, went to their hotel rooms and turned in.

***

The next morning, they took just enough time to have breakfast, and buy some more beef jerky from the mercantile. On a whim, they also bought some cans of peaches, but still no coffee.

"More cold camps," Pike said, "but maybe sweeter ones."

"That's for sure," Clint said, stuffing the peaches into his saddlebags.

They mounted up.

"I wonder if we'll come to another telegraph key before Council Bluffs," Pike commented.

"I hope so," Clint said. "I'd like to find out what's happening in D.C., now."

"I told you my boss, Giles, is a politician. He's going to do whatever he can to mollify the French government. That probably means sending some federal marshals to Council Bluffs."

"If that happens, hopefully they won't show their badges off on the main streets. If the kidnappers see them, they might decide to just finish Verne."

"With two hundred thousand at stake? I think they'll try to make it work. Are you sure there's only two of them?"

"No, I'm not," Clint said. "There were two on the train, but by now there could be more."

"Well, the only place Giles can send federal marshals is Council Bluffs. If they stop somewhere between here and there, it'll just be you and me."

Clint smiled.

"Which means we'll have them right where we want them."

Pike shook his head and grinned.

***

"What's our next stop?" Partridge asked Train, as they drank coffee around the fire before starting out for the day. Verne was on the other side of the fire, also drinking coffee.

"Well, I'll tell you one thing," Train said. "It ain't gonna be Council Bluffs.

"Why not?" Partridge asked. "It's got a telegraph, and it's got a bank. Ain't we gonna need a bank?"

"You wanna collect the ransom and put it in the bank?"

"No," Partridge said, "but I thought we'd probably have to pick the money up from a bank."

"We're not goin' near Council Bluffs," Train said. "Adams is likely to have federal marshals waitin' there."

"I don't wanna go up against no federal marshals," Partridge said.

"Neither do I, but once Adams tells Washington D.C. what's goin' on, whatayou think they're gonna do?"

"Send marshals to Council Bluffs?"

"It's the biggest town near here," Train said. "They'll probably be expectin' us to use it as a ransom drop—just like you were thinkin'."

"But we ain't?"

"No," Train said, "we ain't." I told you, Sam, I always got a plan."

"You wanna let me in on it?"

"Not yet," Train said.

"I have a thought," Verne said to them.

Both men looked across the fire at the writer who, despite being on the trail for days, managed to still look nattily turned out.

"What's that?" Train asked.

"Let me ask for the money," Verne said. "I can contact a representative of my country in Washington."

"You can send a telegram to another Frenchie in Washington?" Partridge asked.

"*Oui*," Verne said, "it will show them that I am alive and well. They will pay the money for my return."

"Are you sure?" Train asked.

"Oh, *oui*, I am very sure," Verne said. "I am very important to zem."

Train leaned forward.

"Can you contact someone from your country without anyone from our government knowin' it?"

"*Oui*," Verne said, "I will send the telegram directly to my countrymen in the French consulate. In fact, I can get a message to the consul general."

Train looked at Partridge.

"We may not have to worry about federal marshals," he said. "Maybe we can do this directly with Frenchie's people."

"But wouldn't they tell somebody in Washington what's goin' on?"

Train looked at Verne.

"What about it, Frenchie?" he asked. "Will your people keep this to themselves?"

"Oh, *Oui*," Verne said. "Since I have been kidnapped in America by Americans, my people will trust no one in your government."

"There you go," Train said to Partridge.

"Great," Partridge said, "now all we need is a place to hold up so this can happen."

"I think I've got just the place," Train said.

Chapter Forty-One

Clint and Pike passed several more towns that were too small to be of any help to them, or the kidnappers. They camped for the night, ate jerky for supper and peaches for breakfast the next morning.

"There's got to be another decent sized town between here and Council Bluffs," Pike said.

"I've been this way before, but these towns pop up and disappear just as quickly."

"I had another thought."

"What's that?"

"Do you think Mr. Verne will try to escape from them?"

"I kind of hope not."

"Why?"

"Because then we'll have absolutely no idea where he is," Clint said. "Right now we figure he's with them, and he's valuable to them. If he tries to escape, they might just shoot him."

"And if he does get away, they'll have to go looking for him."

"And then none of us will know where he is," Clint said. "We want him to be with them when we catch up to them."

"If we catch up to them."

"*When* we do," Clint said. "I'm not going through all of this for nothing."

***

"You see what I see?" Clint asked.

"Where?" Pike asked.

"There." Clint pointed.

Pike squinted.

"I don't see anything."

Clint pointed again.

"Telegraph lines."

"Are they the ones that go to Elk Horn?" Pike asked.

"I don't think so," Clint said. "They're not heading in that direction."

Pike squinted, again.

"I still don't see them," he said, "but I trust your eyesight. Should we go have a look?"

Clint looked down at the tracks they were following.

"It'll take us off the trail," Clint said, "but we could use a telegraph."

"So then, they didn't see these lines, either," Pike said. "They're still heading toward Council Bluffs."

They started riding in the direction Clint had pointed.

"If they don't find another telegraph key they'll have to go all the way to Council Bluffs," Pike said. "That could be a mess."

"Well then, hopefully we can get to a key before that happens," Clint said, "and find out what Washington is planning to do."

"Believe me," Pike said, "they're planning to make a big mess. It's what they always do."

"Let's hope we can head them off."

***

About a half hour later Pike said, "This can't be right."

"It's what it looks like," Clint said. "The telegraph lines go right to that ranch."

"How can a rancher have his own telegraph key?"

"When the rancher has money," Clint said, "they usually think they can have anything they want." He turned his head to follow the lines the other way. "I think these lines probably intersect with the one that goes to Elk Horn."

"Maybe," Pike said, "this ranch spliced into the main line illegally."

"Why don't we go and find out?"

They started down the hill toward the large ranch house.

***

As they approached, they saw two barns, one on either side of a large corral, and two bunkhouses behind it. There was another long building that could have been a mess hall.

"This is a large outfit," Pike said.

"I've never been this way before," Clint said. "And if I hadn't spotted those telegraph wires, this place would have been hidden from sight."

"Makes the telegraph line being illegal that much more likely."

"If that's the case," Clint said, "we're going to have to convince them to let us use it. We might have to bring your identification into play, again."

They rode up to the house, attracting the attention of ranch hands in the corral, and around the mess hall. A couple of men came walking over to them.

"Help you fellas?" one asked.

"We'd like to see the owner, if he's around," Clint said.

"About what?"

"His telegraph key."

The two men exchanged a glance.

"Are you the foreman?" Clint asked.

"Top hand," the man said.

"Is the foreman around?"

"He is."

"Then we might as well start with him."

The top hand turned to the other man and said, "Go get Mack."

"Right."

As the man hurried toward the mess building the man said, "My name's Leo Franks. The foreman's name is Tom MacDougal. Everybody calls him Mack."

"This is Jeremy Pike," Clint said, "and I'm Clint Adams."

Franks stiffened when he heard the name.

"The Gunsmith?"

"That's right."

Franks put his hand on his hip, but he wasn't wearing a gun.

"You ain't here . . . lookin' for somebody, are you?" he asked. "One of our hands?"

"No," Clint said, "we were riding by, and saw the telegraph lines. We're in need of a key."

"There's one in Elk Horn," Franks said. "Another in Council Bluffs, which is less than a day away."

"Is there another one somewhere?" Pike asked.

"Those are the two closest."

"Then it's a good thing we spotted this one," Clint said.

"The boss doesn't let anyone use it," Franks said.

"And who's the boss?"

"His name's Randy Roberts. This is his ranch, the Double-R."

"And I assume this is Mack, coming our way," Clint said.

Franks turned and saw the man he had sent for the foreman returning with a big man.

"What the hell is goin' on?" the big man roared.

Chapter Forty-Two

Clint and Pike dismounted and introduced themselves. Pike also showed his identification.

"The Gunsmith and a government man," the foreman said. "What brings you here?"

"Your telegraph line," Clint said.

"That's private."

"I need to contact Washington," Pike said. "I understand it's private, but I can—"

"Not without a warrant," MacDougal said.

"Do you really want to bring the law into this?" Clint asked.

"Why not?" MacDougal asked. "The line's legal."

"Is it?" Pike asked.

"Yes," MacDougal said. "Look—okay, I suppose you should talk to Mr. Roberts."

"That sounds like a good idea," Clint said.

"Come with me," MacDougal said, and started toward the main house.

He went up the stairs to the front door, with Clint and Pike following.

"Should I put their horses in the barn?" Franks called out.

MacDougal looked at Clint and Pike.

"No," Clint said, "leave them there."

"Then I'll tie off the big one—" the top hand said, grabbing the Darley's reins.

"No," Clint said. "Leave him. He won't go anywhere."

Franks shrugged and dropped Eclipse's reins.

Inside Clint and Pike found themselves in a large, high-ceilinged entry hall, with a large staircase ahead of them.

"Wait here," MacDougal said. "I'll tell the boss you're here."

"I guess you were right," Pike said, as the man left them.

"About what?"

"The money," Pike said. "This is some house, out here in the middle of nowhere. It must've cost a fortune just to get the materials hauled out here to build it."

"I suppose," Clint said, "not to mention getting your own telegraph line."

"I didn't even know a private citizen could do that," Pike said.

"It's money," Clint said. "It always comes down to money."

MacDougal returned.

"The boss said to bring you in," he said. "Follow me."

They followed him down a hall to an open door. They expected to see a telegraph key when they entered, but instead it was a room full of packed bookshelves. There was an armchair in the center, and a man seated there. He was in his sixties, white-haired and, though seated, they could tell he was not tall. He was wearing a bathrobe over a shirt and pants. His feet were bare.

"Mack has told me what you want," the man said.

"Yes," Pike said, "we need to use your telegraph key."

"You can't," Roberts said. "I had Mack bring you in here so I could tell you personally."

"Why do you have your own key?" Clint asked.

"I'm a sick man," Roberts said. "Sometimes I need to contact my doctor immediately. For that reason, I was able to legally acquire a telegraph key."

"And?" Clint asked.

"And I donated a lot of money," Roberts added.

Clint nodded with some satisfaction. It was money.

"Where's your doctor?" Pike asked.

"Elk Horn," Roberts said. "Near Elk Horn, but when I send a telegram there he gets it quickly."

"So why can't we use the key?" Clint asked.

"I need to keep it open," Roberts said. "Sometimes Dr. Neal sends me a telegram. Also, I never know from one minute to the next if I'll need to send him one."

"Look," Pike said, "we're working on a kidnapping, and I need to contact Washington D.C."

"Go to Council Bluffs," Roberts said.

"It may be too late by the time we get there," Pike said.

"I'm sorry," Roberts said. "I can't help."

"I could get a warrant," Pike said.

"That will take time," Roberts said. "On the other hand, you're the Gunsmith. You could force me to let you use it."

"I'd rather not do it that way," Clint said.

"We better get moving," Pike said.

They both turned to leave.

"Just out of curiosity," Roberts said. "who was kidnapped?"

"A man named Jules Verne," Clint said.

As they started out the door Roberts shouted, "Wait!"

They turned, saw him get out of the chair and move quickly to a shelf. He took a book down and showed it to them. It was *20,000 LEAGUES UNDER THE SEA.*

"This Jules Verne?"

"Yes," Clint said, "that one."

Roberts turned and looked at his foreman.

"Take them to the telegraph room," he told him. "Let them use it for as long as it takes."

Chapter Forty-Three

Not only were they permitted to use the telegraph key and operator, but a woman brought in coffee and sandwiches for them, as well.

"I guess we should have mentioned Verne's name as soon as we saw all the books," Clint commented.

Pike nodded, not looking up from the telegram he was writing.

"Okay, that should do it," he said, handing it to the young key operator. "I'm asking what they're doing and at the same time suggesting what they should do."

"Which is?" Clint asked.

"Leave it to us."

"Is that likely?"

"No," Pike said, as the operator began working the key.

Clint and Pike each grabbed a sandwich and washed it down with coffee. Pike was fairly certain somebody in Washington was waiting to hear from them and would answer almost immediately.

He was right.

No sooner had the operator stopped, when his key began chattering away at them.

"Somebody's burnin' up this key," the operator said.

Pike and Clint exchanged a glance. Clint knew he had no problem going against the government, but Pike had to remember who he worked for. Depending on what was being sent, this could signal a parting of the ways for them. Clint knew that Jim West would have stuck with him no matter what, but he didn't know Pike as well.

The operator started writing, trying to keep up with the clacking of the key.

"Here ya go," the operator said, handing Pike the telegram.

Pike put the remainder of his sandwich down and read it.

"They want us to meet up with federal marshals in Council Bluffs," Pike said to Clint.

"That's what we were afraid of," Clint said. "Ask them to give us two more days before they send marshals in."

"What do you expect we'll get done in two days?" Pike asked.

"Well, for one thing," Clint said, "if we end up going all the way to Council Bluffs, we'll get there before the marshals. And if we get there, it'll mean we followed the kidnapper's tracks there. Who knows what can happen?"

"No harm in asking," Pike said, with a shrug.

He wrote out another, shorter message this time and gave it to the key operator.

The reply came back in what sounded like angry clicks.

"Not a chance," Pike said, reading it. "They want me to put you under arrest if I have to, but they want the marshals to handle it."

"Do they say if they've heard anything from the kidnappers?" Clint asked. "Or the French government?"

"No," Pike said, "but it's curious that they're not asking if you've heard from them about the ransom."

"That's true," Clint said. "That could mean they're not worried about the ransom because they don't intend to pay it."

"Well," Pike said, "they're very fond in Washington of saying they won't negotiate with criminals."

"Great," Clint said. "So no money."

"Unless it comes from the French government."

"The only person I know of who could contact the French government is Verne, himself."

"Do you think he's that sharp that he'd get the kidnappers to let him do that?"

"Either he's that smart," Clint said, "or they're that dumb"

"You know," Pike said, "if both governments are involved, this could turn into a huge mess."

"With Jules Verne paying the price," Clint added.

"Well," Randy Roberts said from the doorway, "we can't have that. I think I might be able to help."

Chapter Forty-Four

"That's the place," Train said, pointing.

"It's a shack," Partridge said.

"It'll do," Train told him.

They rode to it and dismounted. When they got inside Partridge saw it looked better than it had from the outside. And there were some supplies.

"What is this?" he asked.

"This was where we were gonna hold up after we hit the train," Train said. "Now you're gonna stay here with Frenchie while I go to Council Bluffs and get our money."

Partridge stared at Train for a few moments.

"What?" Train asked. "You don't trust me to come back with the money?"

"It's two hundred thousand dollars, Dan," Partridge said.

"And we're splittin' it fifty-fifty, Sam," Train said. "A hundred thousand is a lot of money. I'm satisfied with that."

Partridge looked over at Jules Verne, who cocked an eyebrow at him.

"I still believe I should go wiz you," Verne said.

"That's okay, Frenchie," Train said. "You just tell me who to contact among your Frenchie buddies in Washington. I'll take care of it."

"How far are we from Council Bluffs?" Partridge asked.

"About an hour."

"Then why don't we all ride in?"

"Because if Adams is there, or if marshals are there, they'll be lookin' for three of us. It's safer for you and Frenchie to stay here. Now, come on outside for a minute."

Partridge stepped outside the shack with Train.

"You're gonna be here overnight with Frenchie," Train told him. "Make sure you tie him up."

"Yeah, okay."

"And don't kill 'im unless you have to."

"Why would I have to?" Partridge asked.

"Why did you have to kill the old guy in the livery?" Train asked.

"I told you that was an accident!"

"Yeah, you stabbed him by accident," Train said. "Just don't get too excited, okay?"

"When we get the money we're gonna give him back, right?" Partridge asked.

"Let's see what happens before we make any decisions," Train said. "Just make sure he's here and alive when I get back."

"You are comin' back, right?"

"Sam," Train said. "I'll be back. But if I'm not back in a couple of days, it'll probably mean I got caught, or killed."

"Jeez, then what do I do?" Partridge asked.

"At that point," Train said, "you'll be on your own. Whatever you do then will be up to you."

Train walked to his horse and mounted up.

"Remember," he said, "just stay calm."

As Train rode away, Partridge wondered if he would ever see him again. When he went inside, Jules Verne voiced the man's own thought.

"Do you zink we will ever see him again?" the writer asked. "After all, he will have two hundred zousand dollars."

"You really think your Frenchies are gonna pay that much for you?"

"Oh, *Mon ami*," Jules Verne said, "they would probably pay more."

"Well then," Partridge said, "if he doesn't come back with the money, I'll still have you, won't I?"

"Oh, indeed," Verne said, "you will still have me."

"Then shut up," Partridge said, "and make yourself useful. Put on a pot of coffee."

***

"It's no go," Pike said, handing Clint the telegram. "They're sending marshals to Council Bluffs."

"Then we'll have to hope we can catch up to the kidnappers before they get there," Clint said. "We still have some daylight to pick up their trail again."

"Let's see what our host has in mind," Pike said. "It can't hurt."

Roberts had told his foreman to bring Clint and Pike back to the library after they finished with the telegraph key. When they got there, he was sitting in his chair with Verne's book opened in his lap.

"Ah, any luck?" he asked.

"Just the bad kind," Clint said. "The federal marshals are going to rush in and make a mess of things."

"Maybe I can help," Roberts said.

"How?" Clint asked.

"I know some people in Washington," the rancher said. "If you and Pike start after the kidnappers again, maybe I can buy you some time with a few well-placed telegrams."

"You could do that?" Clint asked.

"I can try," Roberts said. "But there's a condition."

"What is it?" Clint asked.

"After you save him," Roberts said, "I want to meet Jules Verne."

Clint approached the man, stuck his hand out to shake, and said, "You've got it."

Chapter Forty-Five

When Clint and Pike rode into Council Bluffs the following day they wondered about the federal marshals.

"You think Roberts will be able to do what he said?" Clint asked.

"I think so," Pike said.

"Why?"

"I know what goes on in Washington," Pike said. "Roberts is going to flex some muscles. That means money. You may not like that, but in this case, it could help us."

As they rode in no one seemed to be paying them any special attention.

"No marshals," Clint said.

"How do you know?"

"If they had ridden in, they would have attracted attention," Clint said. "And so would we. It's been quiet here."

"That's good," Pike said. "There's the telegraph office."

"Let's check it."

They reined in their horses in front of the office and entered.

"Have any strangers been in here sending a telegram to Washington D.C., or Des Moines?" Pike asked.

"Who wants to know?" the middle-aged clerk asked.

Pike showed the man his identification.

"Oh," the clerk said, "well, yeah, there was a fella in here last night. He sent one to Washington."

"Did he get an answer?"

"Yes."

"We'd like to see both telegrams."

"Uh, I don't have them," the clerk said. "The man took them with him."

"What about our copies?"

"Those, too."

"Are you supposed to do that?"

"No."

"Then why did you?" Clint asked.

"He threatened me. I wasn't willing to die for some pieces of paper."

Pike didn't comment.

"Good call," Clint said.

"Thanks."

"Do you remember what the telegrams said?" Clint asked.

"Yes."

***

Clint and Pike found the kidnapper in a saloon called The Wagon Wheel. He looked up at them as they approached his table.

"I wondered when you'd get here," he said. "Have a seat."

"Which one are you?" Clint asked. "Train or Partridge?"

"I'm Dan Train," the man said.

"Kind of ironic, don't you think?" Pike asked. "That you were planning to rob a train?"

"Yeah, I got that." Train rolled his eyes.

"Where's Mr. Verne?" Clint asked.

"He's safe."

"Alive?" Pike asked.

Train nodded.

"And safe."

"But not here in town," Clint said.

"No," Train said, "I'm not that stupid. Stupid enough to leave a trail you could follow, but not that stupid."

Pike and Clint exchanged a look.

"Oh yeah, I know you think we were dumb," Train said, "but you're here, and there are no marshals, are there?"

"No," Pike said, "apparently not yet."

"I didn't know who I'd have to deal with when I decided to ride in here," Train said. "But I'm kind of glad it's you, Adams." He looked at Pike. "And who are you?"

"Secret Service."

"Ah. Well, I sent a telegram to Washington."

"To the French embassy," Clint said.

"The clerk told you," Train said. "I thought he might. Yeah, they wanna give me the money."

"When the U.S. government learns of this, they'll step in," Pike said.

"Since there are no marshals here, I assume they haven't heard yet?" Train said. "You musta done somethin' to keep it from them. I think I can get the money from the Frenchies before that happens—with your help."

"What makes you think we'll help you get the money?" Clint asked.

"You want Frenchie alive, right? And back?"

"Yes."

"Pay me, and you can have him." Train took a piece of paper from his pocket. "The Frenchies said you should contact them, and they'll let you have the money to give to me." He handed Clint the telegram.

"That's what it says, all right," Clint said, handing it to Pike.

"Then you better get to that," Train said. "We wanna get it done before the marshals ride in."

Chapter Forty-Six

Train told them to get the money and bring it to him in the Wagon Wheel.

"Right here, in front of people?" Pike asked.

"Can you think of a better place?" Train asked. "Maybe in an alley, where you can kill me instead if givin' me the money?"

"We're not going to kill you," Pike said. "If we have to, we'll give you the money."

"No," Clint said.

"What?" Train asked.

"I won't give you the money in here, or in town," Clint said. "You'll take us to Jules Verne. When I see he's okay, I'll give you the money, and you'll give us him. That's how it's going to work."

"Do you think you're callin' this play, Adams?" Train asked.

"No, I don't think that," Clint said. "I know it. You took Mr. Verne from me. You'll get the money when you give him back to me."

Train looked at Pike, who simply shrugged.

"Okay," Train said. "You bring the money here, show it to me, and then we'll go and get Frenchie."

Clint and Pike stood up.

"If he's been hurt," Clint said, "or if your partner killed him the way he killed the hostler in Des Moines, I'll kill the both of you."

"Understood," Train said.

***

"You think I played it wrong?" Clint asked Pike as they stepped outside.

"No," Pike said. "I think you played it exactly right. We better send that telegram to the French embassy in Washington."

"And some others," Clint said.

***

They went to the telegraph office and the clerk was happy to help them. He was hoping they wouldn't turn him in for what he did with Train's telegrams.

Clint sent the telegram to the French embassy about the money. He then sent a telegram to Randy Roberts' key, and finally had Pike send a telegram to his boss.

"We'll need replies as soon as they come in," Clint told the clerk.

"Where will you be?"

"Right outside."

Clint and Pike left the office. There were chairs out front, four of them. They pulled two up against the wall and sat in them.

"You know," Pike said, "if we see marshals riding down the street, we're going to be in trouble."

"We could back track his trail, try to follow it back to wherever he'd left his partner and Verne."

"We'd have to find his horse, and start from there," Pike said. "Work backwards, like you say. Can you do that?"

"Maybe," Clint said. "Probably."

"Fast enough?" Pike went on. "Before Train realizes we're trying to go around him?"

"Maybe," Clint said again, then, "maybe not."

"Then let's get the money, and get Mr. Verne back," Pike said. "After that if you want to try and track them and retrieve the money, you can."

"Or we could force him to take us," Clint said.

"Can we?" Pike asked. "He's not as dumb as we might have thought. Maybe he's braver than we think, too."

"In that case we've got to stick to our plan," Clint said.

"Which keeps changing," Pike said.

"With the French involved maybe our government will back off and let us work," Clint said.

"We'll find out as soon as we get a reply," Pike pointed out.

They sat back in their chairs to wait, but not patiently.

***

Dan Train was not happy.

He had never intended to go back to the shack where he'd left Partridge and Frenchie. His plan was to collect the money, then tell Adams—or whoever—where they were. Then Frenchie would be recovered, Partridge would take the rap, and Train would be gone with the money. Right from the beginning of this kidnap plan he intended to leave Partridge holding the bag.

Now that had changed.

He was going to have to figure out how to handle the government man and the Gunsmith. The only way he figured to do that was to use the French writer as a shield. There still had to be a way for him to get away with the money and leave Partridge behind to take the rap.

Nobody knew how smart he really was, not even Partridge, or any of the partners he had worked with in the past. That meant he was always being underestimated. Hopefully, that was what he could use to his advantage against the Gunsmith.

That and a few other things.

Chapter Forty-Seven

The clerk came out three times, each time handing them a telegram.

"Roberts kept his word," Pike said, handing the first telegram to Clint. "He's managed to get our government to hold off on the marshals."

"I don't know how he did it, but at least we won't have to deal with a bunch of badge toters messing things up."

"If I'm not mistaken" Pike said, "there was a time you toted a badge, yourself."

"Years ago," Clint said, "before I smartened up."

Since Pike was sitting by the door, the clerk handed him the telegrams when he came out.

"My boss isn't happy, but he says there won't be any marshals here until tomorrow. So he's giving us twenty-four hours to get Verne back."

"Suits me," Clint said. "It's not like we're still looking for the kidnappers."

"No," Pike said, "we're just looking for the kid-napee."

"And the French?" Clint asked.

"Take a look," Pike said. "It's addressed to you, any-way." He handed it over.

Clint read, and said, "We can pick the money up at the local bank."

"They've got that much on hand?"

"They went to work on this right away," Clint said. "Apparently, the cash was delivered to the bank yesterday."

"We might as well go and get it, then," Pike said, "before somebody decides to rob the bank. That much money can't have come in without someone knowing about it."

"Carrying that much money," Clint said, as they stood, "we're going to have big bullseyes on our backs."

"That shouldn't be anything new for you," Pike observed.

***

"Do you want us to send some guards with you?" the bank manager asked.

They were in his office, with the money sacked on his desk. Clint and Pike started stuffing the bills into their saddlebags, rather than walk out of the bank carrying money bags.

"No, that's okay," Clint said. "We've got it."

"This is a lot of money," the manager said, nervously. "I don't mind telling you, it's made us all quite nervous to have it here."

"Well," Pike said, "hopefully those nerves didn't cause anybody to talk about it."

"Oh, of course not," the manager said. "Our staff is very reliable."

"That's good," Clint said, tossing his saddlebags over his shoulder.

"But," the manager said, as Pike did the same and they started for the door, "what about notifying the sheriff?"

"We will," Clint said, "after."

"For now," Pike said, "we need you and your staff to stay inside, and stay reliable, huh?"

"Oh, yes, sir."

Clint and Pike left with the money.

***

Out in front of the bank they looked up and down the street to be sure no one was showing any interest in them. Then they tossed the saddlebags onto their mounts, and started walking the horses over to the Wagon Wheel Saloon.

***

Dan Train's heart began to beat faster as he saw Clint Adams and Jeremy Pike enter the saloon carrying saddlebags—bulging saddlebags.

"Are you ready?" Clint asked him.

"Let's see it."

Clint and Pike looked around, then sat so they would attract less attention from the others in the saloon—not that there were that many. Just a few men, standing at the bar or seated at tables.

Clint pushed his saddlebags over to Train, who opened them and looked inside at the cash.

"The same amount in those saddlebags?" he asked Pike.

"Yes."

Clint pulled the saddlebags back.

"Now it's time for you to keep your end of the bargain," he said.

"Oh yeah," Train said, raising his voice, "my end of the bargain."

Suddenly, the other men in the Wagon Wheel moved, leaving the bar, rising from their tables, and came closer.

"These men are here to help me keep my end," Train told them.

Clint and Pike looked around. No wonder he wanted to receive the money here, and not out in the open.

Clint counted eight men, all wearing side arms.

Chapter Forty-Eight

"Is he paying you?" Clint asked. "From his ransom money?" He put his hand on the saddlebags. "Do any of you know how much is in here?"

"They don't have to know," Train said, standing. "They're being paid."

He grabbed for the saddlebags, but Clint would not release his, and Pike held tightly to his.

"It's not going to be that easy, Train," Clint said.

"Do these men know who they're facing?" Pike asked. "A representative of the United States Secret Service? And the Gunsmith?"

A murmur went up from the surrounding men.

"So he's the Gunsmith," Train said, loudly. "He's only one man."

"One man," Clint said, raising his own voice, "with six bullets. That means six of you die."

"That leaves three to kill you," Train said.

"No," Pike said. "I'm not the gunman the Gunsmith is, but with six bullets of my own, I can kill three men."

Clint looked over at the bartender.

"Are you in on this?"

The bartender shook his head.

"I'm just serving drinks."

"Let go of my money!" Train snapped.

"If you want it," Clint said, holding onto his saddlebags with his left hand, "take it."

But Clint didn't wait for Train to make up his mind. Or for the eight men to decide if they wanted to fight or run. Normally, he gave men the opportunity to make up their own minds.

Not this time.

He drew his gun and fired.

Pike, seeing Clint, draw, produced his own weapon.

Train hit the floor, taking cover underneath the table. When Clint and Pike were dead, he'd take his money.

Some of the other eight men in the room were taken aback, surprised that Clint Adams would draw on eight men. They reacted slowly.

Others reacted quickly, so it was easy for Clint to choose his targets. And he did something he rarely did. He fanned the hammer on his Colt, slapping it back with his left hand again, and again. This was a wildly erratic way to fire a gun, for the pressure of the hand striking the hammer jerked the barrel up. But the Gunsmith knew how to do it, and keep his barrel steady.

Men fell, like ten pins.

Pike drew his own weapon and fired as the remainder of the men did the same. He felt a bullet tug at his sleeve, but kept pulling his trigger until his gun was empty.

And it grew silent.

The air smelled of cordite and gun smoke.

Clint looked around, saw eight men lying on the floor. Quickly, he ejected the spent shells from his gun and looked at Pike.

"Are you all right?"

Pike looked at his sleeve, the one with the hole in it. The bullet had only gone through the cloth, not his arm.

"I'm fine. Where's Train?"

Clint pointed down to the table.

"Train, come on out," he said. "Leave your gun behind. It's over."

Train stuck his head up from beneath the table, looked around in disbelief.

"Fuck," he said.

"If you stand up with your gun, I'll kill you."

"You kill me you won't find Frenchie," Train said.

"We'll keep looking," Clint said. "We'll find him and your partner. Maybe we'll even give him the money."

Train grabbed for a saddlebag with his left hand, but Clint pulled it back.

"The money's mine!" Train shouted.

"Like we agreed," Clint said. "Take us to Jules Verne, and the money's yours."

"Still?" Train asked. He looked around at the dead men, then stood slowly. Clint noticed his gun was not in his holster. "You're not gonna kill me?"

"No," Clint said.

Pike's empty shells hit the floor. He reloaded and holstered his gun.

"We intend to keep our part of the bargain," he said. "But we have to get out of here now, before the local law arrives. Or we'll have a lot of explaining to do."

"You gonna leave all these dead men in my place?" the bartender asked.

"You explain what happened to the sheriff," Clint said. "Tell him we'll be back."

"Who's gonna pay for all the damage?"

There was broken glass everywhere from the bottles and mirror behind the bar.

Clint smiled and pointed at Dan Train.

"He is," he said.

Chapter Forty-Nine

Sam Partridge and Jules Verne were eating bacon-and-beans when they heard horses approaching.

"Stay!" Partridge said, as Verne started to rise. "Or I'll tie you up, again."

He stood and went to the window with his hand on his gun.

"It's Train," he said, "with two men."

"Is one of them Clint Adams?" Verne asked. "Has he come for me?"

"I can't tell." Partridge turned. "You stay in here until I call you."

"As you wish." Verne stuffed his mouth with bacon-and-beans, some of it dripping onto his beard. He felt he was eating like a Westerner.

Partridge opened the front door and stepped out. He waited for the three men to get closer. As they did he recognized Clint Adams from the train. He didn't know the other man.

"Do you have the money?" he called out to Train.

But it wasn't Train who answered, it was Clint Adams.

"Do you have Jules Verne?"

"He's here."

"Is he all right?"

"He's fine."

"Let us see him."

Partridge looked at Train.

"Why's he doin' all the talkin'?"

Train didn't answer, just looked sullen.

"He's our prisoner," Clint said. "He tried to ambush us with eight men, take the money and leave. He never had any intention of coming back here."

Partridge looked at Train again.

"Is that true?"

Train didn't answer.

"He's a little depressed at the moment," Clint said. "You can see he has no gun. And now I have to ask you to put down yours."

Partridge reached behind him and opened the door.

"Frenchie!"

Verne came outside. Immediately, Partridge pointed his gun at the writer.

"Where's the money?" he asked Clint.

"In our saddlebags."

"Toss them down."

Clint tossed his to the ground, followed by Pike's.

"Go get them," he said to Verne.

"Stand still, Jules," Clint said. To Partridge: "You get them."

"I'll shoot 'im!" Partridge threatened.

"And then we'll shoot you," Clint said, "pick up the money, and leave."

"What about Train?"

"We'll give him to the law."

Partridge frowned, trying to understand.

"While you're making up your mind," Clint said, "why doesn't Jules go and get his horse?"

"What about him?" Partridge asked, indicating Train with his gun hand. "Was he really gonna light out with the money?"

"And leave you to take the rap," Clint said. "Yeah."

"Sam, look—" Train started, but Partridge cut him off by shooting him in the chest. Train went over backward and hit the ground with a dull thud. Dead.

Partridge looked at Jules Verne.

"Go get your horse."

***

"Mr. Randy Roberts," Clint said, "meet Jules Verne."

Verne entered the library and shook hands with the rancher, who was still wearing a robe.

"Oh my God," Roberts said, "This is an honor. Are you, uh, all right?"

"I need a bath," Verne said, "and a good meal, but *oui*, I am good. I have seen your West as I never expected to see it."

"I will have a bath drawn for you," Roberts said, "and when you come out there'll be a meal waiting."

"Not beans?" Verne asked.

Roberts laughed.

"Definitely not beans."

He looked past Verne at Clint and Pike, who were in the doorway.

"Can we use the telegraph?" Clint asked. "We've got one of the kidnappers with us, and we need to notify the marshals so they can come and get him."

"Of course," Roberts said, "and when you're finished, there'll be a hot meal waiting for all of you."

"Except the kidnapper," Clint said, "who also happens to be a killer. We need someplace to put him."

"There's a shed in the back," Roberts said, "with a good, strong lock. I'll have Mack take you back there."

"Thank you, Mr. Roberts," Clint said, "for everything."

"Hey," the rancher said, pointing at Jules Verne, "you kept your part of the bargain."

As Roberts led Verne out of the room Clint stopped the writer and said, "I'm sorry."

"For what?"

"For letting you get kidnapped."

"It was an experience I never would have had if I had not met you," Verne said, "so zank you."

He followed Roberts down the hall.

"That's quite a fella," Jeremy Pike said.

"Sure is," Clint said. "Let's contact the marshals and get this over with."

As they turned to go Pike said, "After his experience in our Wild West, you think he'll write about it?"

"I don't know," Clint said, "but if he does, I hope he doesn't include me."

"Why not?"

"Too many books written about me already," Clint said.

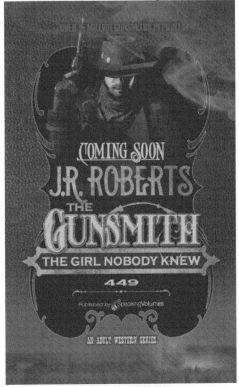

Coming Soon!

Lady Gunsmith 7
Roxy Doyle and the James Boys

For more information
visit: www.SpeakingVolumes.us

On Sale Now!

ANGEL EYES *series*
by Award-Winning Author
Robert J. Randisi (J.R. Roberts)

For more information
visit: www.SpeakingVolumes.us

Made in the USA
Middletown, DE
16 July 2019